My Life in Receipts

Andrew Dutton

LEAF BY LEAF

Published by Leaf by Leaf
an imprint of Cinnamon Press,
Office 49019, PO Box 15113, Birmingham, B2 2NJ
www.cinnamonpress.com

The right of Andrew Dutton to be identified as author of this work has been asserted by him in accordance with the Copyright, Designs and Patent Act, 1988. © 2023, Andrew Dutton.
Print Edition ISBN 978-1-78864-983-4
British Library Cataloguing in Publication Data. A CIP record for this book can be obtained from the British Library.

All rights reserved. No part of this publication may be reproduced, stored in a retrieval system, or in any form or by any means, electronic, mechanical, photocopying, recording or otherwise without the prior written permission of the publishers. This book may not be lent, hired out, resold or otherwise disposed of by way of trade in any form of binding or cover other than that in which it is published, without the prior consent of the publishers.

Designed and typeset in Adobe Caslon by Cinnamon Press.
Cover design by Adam Craig © Adam Craig
Cinnamon Press is represented by Inpress.

Acknowledgements

Quotation from 'England 1-2 Iceland: Euro 2016—as it happened' by courtesy of Guardian News & Media Ltd.

To 'McLennan',
and all those who keep up the fight.

My Life in Receipts

LSD and the Lost Generation

Two and two
Is twenty-four
Shut your gob
And say no more!

We chanted in the playground, led by Julie Fagin, class badgirl. It was in protest to, release from, parroting times-tables, standing to attention at our desks—faces raised, as if offering fervent prayer, but for the odd fact we were told to keep our arms stiff at our sides like soldiers.

Those numbers, hummed, almost plain-sung, were meant to worm themselves into our minds, irremovable, but to this chanson I was tone-deaf; it was 1968, my first year at school, and I was already encountering what someone would—much later—pin close as 'your outright anathema for mathematics'. It didn't help that two and two did, in their way, make twenty-four, as I found when we began to learn about money. It was all confusing, the LSD system. Pounds were the L (but why?), Shillings the S (fair enough) and Pennies the D.
D?
Why not P?

But what's important is what teacher says; what teacher says is right. Julie Fagin may have queened it in the playground, but it was time to ignore her. *Pay attention!* Nobody wants a child who can be cheated and short-changed with impunity. Nobody wanted to confuse infants with explanations of our Latin-haunted language. *Libra Pondo*; *Solidus*; *Denarius*: evidencing the long, cold reach of an ancient occupier into remote posterity. Grownups had decided this was the system, who were we to argue? *Just learn it.*

They said if you looked after the pennies, the pounds would look after themselves—but it wasn't so. They needed chasing, corralling, counting up, and that was hard, not least because in spite of us having ten fingers to work with, money didn't work so handily; it jumped about in threes, sixes, twelves… twenty-fours.

Twelve pennies made a shilling.

The S. was also a Bob.

[Twelve times One is Twelve]

With threepence and sixpence in between—the Joey or Thruppence, and the Tanner.

[Three times one is… two times three is…]

Two shillings was a florin.

[Two times twelve is…]

Two shillings and sixpence—half a crown.

[Twelve times two-and-a half is…]

But the full Crown was unused.

[Twenty-four times two-and-a-half is…]

Ten Bob came in the form of a small brown note.

[Twelve times Ten is…]

Twenty Bob made a pound, the L. 240d. A green note. A quid.

[Twelve times twenty is… twenty four…]

There was a difference between Pounds and Guineas. Nobody told us what it was because Guineas were ancient history, yet people still leaped from one to the other, carelessly causing further muddle.

Why was it so confusing?

Everyday language was full of this; it was woven in. Something cheap but trying to act above its station was 'tuppeny-ha'penny'. Christmas puddings had sixpences buried in them. Some vast, square-shaped six-year-old at school threatened me, fat fist raised, with 'a fourpenny one'. My pocket money was the Saturday Sixpence. Someone would make a silly bet of a 'tanner to a toffee'. My great-grandmother told my skinny Dad he had 'a bum like a ninepenny rabbit'. Half-pennies weren't used anymore. Nor florins or farthings. But they were talked of as though alive. To torment a classmate, a shopkeeper's daughter, Julie F coined the money-tinged ditty:

Karen Gaston sells fish
Three ha'pence a dish
Don't buy em
Don't buy em
They stink when you fry em

She had revived the ha'penny and invented the consumer boycott.

Some coins were undoubtedly pretty, but many looked as if they had been dug from long years in the ground, dull brown discs bearing the profiles of long-dead kings. Coins went out of use from time to time and they seemed to get rid of the prettiest ones—the ha'penny and farthing, the sailing ship and the little wren. But the farthing was half of half a penny and that was too much of too little for me; I was glad it was gone. You could say these things were valuable because they were time-honoured, but... we pay far too much honour to time.

There was no way to get a grip, it was all threes, nines, twelves, twenty-fours: none of it made sense. Other enemies lurked when we came to measure and weigh: fourteens, sixteens, sixteenths; hundredweights that weren't a hundred of anything but twelve more. Pints, quarts, gallons—ones, twos and eights. Feet and inches—sixes and twelves again, this time reacting with threes: *Twelve Times Three* to make a yard. Times another 1760 to make a mile. There were leagues too—multiply your twelve times three times 1760 by another three.

'I think you're a King!' cried Julie Fagin, false-smiling.

'Wh-why?'

'Cos a King's a ruler, a ruler's a foot, a foot smells and so do you! Hahaha!'

My head spun: I was lost. There was more confusion: decisions, about which the grownups weren't telling us. One was a big change, debated and argued for years, decades: our two-and-two struggles had been in vain, understand the system or no. I was eight years of age when the message reached me: 'Stop everything! Forget what we told you over these last three years! It's all changed, it now works in fives and tens: finger-money!'

No more LSD: and, triumph, the D was now a P! The penny, once bigger than more valuable coins, shrank to a commensurate tininess; the halfpenny was back—smaller still—though not for long. Three pence was no longer 'thruppence' or dignified with its own coin, it had no special place or name and 'three' became a placeholder between the penny, two pence and five pence pieces—and we said 'five pence' now, not fivepence; an important alteration. Six was demoted to a staging-post between five and ten, 'sixpence' was gone; the coins remained for a time but were valued at two and a half new pence; the mighty shilling was tamed, a humble 5p; the all-important Twelve just an insignificant stop-off between ten and twenty, dominant no longer. Ten shillings was 50p; no longer a note. And it was the same for weights and measures; clean multiples of one-five-ten, no more fourteens, sixteens, sixteenths or hundreds that weren't a hundred.

Forget, unlearn, then learn anew. There were posters on street corners showing the new decimal currency; exciting in its novelty. People complained and said the old folk would never get used to it, the children would be confused by the stop-start, we were creating a lost generation. The thrupenny bit was taken away days after the new money arrived; another pretty coin with multiple sides and a funny gate-thing on one face; it lost its place to a 2p coin. The old penny was gone at the same time too. The rebadged sixpence pieces lingered. There was even a Save The Sixpence campaign, but another old d-coin was lost at last. Fives tens, hundreds, stacking cleanly, easy to understand. Just what I'd asked for. I didn't know who to thank. But I was, I am, confused, the past clings, tenacious, woven into the everyday. My beer comes in pints but my wine in centilitres. I look at a digital display of kilos and reach for the internet to tell me what that means in stones; my expanding waistline is measured in inches. 'Give em an inch and they take a mile'; 'doing the hard yards'; 'acres of space'; 'missed by a mile'; try saying any of those using five-ten-hundred language, try Julie F's 'king' insult; even 'in for a penny, in for a pound', which at least works with the new money, but you know it means the old money.

Those old coins are collectors' items now, and that's not the only nostalgia they generate: some have chafed against the fives and tens for decades, they yearn; they want the old system back, three-six-twelve-twenty-four. Defeat Napoleon, they say, reverse his from-the-grave-conquest of a proud land, roll back time, restore the Romans, they're our kind of conqueror.

And it is to them I say:

Ten times ten
Is twenty-four
Shut your gob
And say no more!

I, Scienteest

It was clear what I was. I looked the part: a small boy with short dark hair, an overly serious expression and thick bubble-eye glasses, the NHS type that consigned their wearers to years of mockery and cries of 'four-eyes!', until they were finally lent a geeky trendiness by a pop star in the mid-80s. Additionally, I played the part; I was fascinated with stars and space, I had a big map of the sky on my bedroom wall, I pored over the reports of the Moon landings long after everyone else—including the inconstant Americans—had got bored with the whole business. I could be found, even on the coldest evenings, peering intently into the eyepiece of my beloved telescope while other kids were cosy indoors, apparently engaged in learning every note and word of the night's adverts on TV. It was plain—I was a boffin, a brainbox; my role in life defined.

It wasn't just the other children who cast me so; I sat in a classroom at my junior school one day, reading *The Story of Astronomy* (£2.50). I had a lot of books like that, I debuted with Ladybird books (2/6d), progressing to bigger-boy books—passing the time doing 'topics' as a PE lesson in the schoolyard had been rained off.

The PE teacher supervising the room of gameless,

largely aimless children, was a bawling bully named Yawton, whose idea of encouraging his young athletes was to employ his coarse voice to yell 'You *clown!*' and other endearments at any youngster who couldn't perform somersaults on his impatient, bellowed command. He too wore glasses, but they sat on a rectangular nose set in a cuboid head sided with sanded-down brown hair; the spectacles did not make him one of my tribe—they were simply there, the better for him to focus upon what he shouted at. As a man of action, Yawton was clearly ill at ease behind a desk, watching over us until we could be sent back to our own classrooms. His restless gaze roamed, efficiently and effectively dousing incipient outbursts of trouble, keeping kiddie-chatter to a minimum.

Having arrived at the room last, I was in the front row, directly before the teacher with my book propped in front of me—I was proud of it, remember—its title easy for Yawton to spy with his little eye. I was aware of him leaning forward to peer at the book, and then me.

'Are you a *scienteest*?' he boomed. The windows shook. Everyone looked up. His tone of mild contempt was, I hazarded, an attempt to be friendly—as close as he passed to the alien concept of friendliness—and, feeling superior in every possible way to this muscle-bound voice-box, I smiled smugly and assented. That was me; it was my destiny.

So, I was ten years old and a scienteest. Had I not been reading about Ptolemy, Aristotle, Archimedes, Copernicus, Galileo, Brahe, Kepler, Hooke, Newton and their ilk, albeit in pop-science books with lots of pictures rather than enormous tomes inscribed in ancient Latin? Had I not sniggered at the foolish fumbling of the ancients as they explored and thoroughly misunderstood nature? Had I not been shocked at the dogmatic refusal of their successors to test their silly, scatter-brained beliefs? Had I not cheered the heroes of invention and discovery as they broke the fetters of ignorance and shed light on the universe's mysteries? Was I not a product of a modern society that honoured science and technology? Surely all I needed in addition to the glasses, books and an attitude of mind was a white coat, lab, set of steaming, bubbling retorts and a rack of test tubes.

To be a true 70s scienteest I should also have possessed a computer, a huge electronic beast occupying the whole wall of a clean white room as it buzzed and chattered, its vast magnetic tapes spinning, the immortal machine performing its science-fiction broodings.

We were taught no science whatsoever at primary school, but that could wait; science was big stuff, clearly not for kiddies. In the meantime, I realised I would probably never be a moon-walking astronaut, but consoled myself that it would be just as exciting to be part of the glow and beep of Mission Control: yes, that was how I would spend my future days. Impatient to attend to my real work, I would imagine my school desk, a dull brown thing that had lost its varnish in a long and apparently catastrophic lifetime, humming with power, its lid turning slowly to reveal an instrument panel crammed with lights and switches, the blackboard becoming a screen on which a rocket's trajectory made an illuminated curve, the room filling with excited voices that called out flight status, checked, rechecked, counted down: I daydreamed the voices of the future.

The Moonshots had come to an end but there were a dozen other exciting projects that would need my skills and enthusiasm—I particularly fancied the 'Grand Tour', which I had read about on a small picture-card given out with packets of tea, a plan to send a robot probe on a series of slingshot orbits planet-by-planet around the solar system, revealing the secrets of the sky. Yes, I would be at Mission Control, receiving high-resolution, highly coloured pictures of our neighbours in space, discussing them with NASA colleagues, then explaining it all on the TV and writing books to entertain and inform a star-struck public and inspire the next generation of eager, bespectacled scienteests.

I never even got my job at Mission Control: but why not, when it had seemed so obvious that this was what life had decided for me? Anathema struck; the scientist and author Lancelot Hogben held that if we don't possess the language of maths, we cannot contribute to the vital conversation about the future of humanity. Cheers, Lance mate, no, really. But alas: that was the problem. From LSD onwards, I suffered from 'The Maths Feeling', a desperate panic-attack that swept over me as soon any attempt was made to take me beyond the safe haven of two-plus-two. It was a true sinking sensation as I realised numbers were not going to open up to me and indeed that the vicious brutes were intent on fighting back—and winning. The Maths Feeling was a horrid variation on the cliché of wading through glue: I was wading through glue with lead in my legs, a ton weight crushing my head, a mouthful of sharp pins and broken glass, and cruel, mocking laughter in my ears. I sank out of sight in the morass—and drowned, every time.

A portent of my doom came in the form of Mr Johns, the sarcastic teacher of Maths Set A, my misbegotten placement in which I had blandly accepted as appropriate homage to my high intelligence. Mr Johns didn't like children who couldn't do maths, especially when they were supposed to be in the top stream. I sat there, a model of mute disbelief: in all my time at school I had never been shouted at by a teacher—dammit I was *clever*—and yet here I was in the front row of Mr Johns' class, oppressed by the Maths Feeling and gazing numbly at him, bovine as he towered over me, projecting his voice to make sure no one in the room missed my humiliation.

'Every time I ask you a question it's the same! It's no use you sitting there looking up to heaven and offering a silent prayer to be sent the right answer! I may as well send you down the corridor to join the remedial class if that's the way you go about things!' I nearly asked him to make good on that threat-promise. Perhaps I should have, but I had lost all courage. I shut up shop, closed down my brain and waited for him, and the underlying problem, to clear off and leave me alone.

The 11-Plus came along and I passed it. There were no maths questions, that I can recall. What mattered to me was that I was headed for the best school in the area, one that taught science in venerable chemistry and biology labs that appeared to have been constructed by the noble founders of those disciplines. Even more excitingly, there was a modern-looking physics block, square, flat-roofed, glassy; science was calling me. I worked out quickly that I was hopeless at certain subjects—woodwork, metalwork, any task for which I had to use my hands—but I was at peace with that, certain subjects were compulsory for the first three years or so and I would shed these burdens when I could. And anyway, I *was* going to be a Mission Controller: problem solved. I had a good start in chemistry: we were taught a little of the history of the science, and I absorbed with alacrity the stories of Lavoisier and Priestley, I sniggered at those who vaunted the discredited Phlogiston theory; silly, silly people, how *could* they have believed such tosh! Science had a narrative, it had goodies and baddies too—yay to the heroes who found the truth, boo to the sillies who got it wrong.

But it wasn't long until I quailed before the unwelcome advent of the evil, bastard twin of the Maths Feeling—the Science-Lesson Feeling: the same bemused, head-scratching lost-boy emptiness. I just didn't know what the teachers were talking about.

Having glasses, short hair and an earnest expression wasn't enough. I despaired of getting my white coat; and by greater gradations, went off the idea of being a scienteest altogether.

A true scientist would never have ignored the accumulation of negative evidence as I had over the years. I had received a chemistry set for one birthday, and my (ab)use of it should have given clear warnings about my clumsiness, my lack of precision and focus, and my disinclination to pay attention to instructions. I burnt a few things, turned others from one colour to another, failed to see the point, got bored, gave up.

Then I had a biology set; I was fascinated by the microscope that was its centrepiece, but I could never see a bloody thing through it, I baulked at dissecting the poor little dead creatures thoughtfully supplied in grim little bottles, broke some of the glass slides and retreated, confused and sheepish.

I also had an electricity kit: the less said the better, but it's relevant to admit I couldn't even light a tiny bulb from a battery, never mind construct the simple circuits suggested in the manual. Although I kept coming back to this thing with apparent indefatigability, my returns were ever more quietly despairing and ended when too many wires, screws and other bits and bobs finally vanished from the flattened, broken-sided box and fell into whatever void lies out there waiting to swallow discarded toys.

I hung on for a time to the sickly hope that I could still be a scienteest –working at Mission Control required no messing with chemistry or biology sets, after all—but then the final, fatal crash came when the figures took over completely and the learning of science became nothing much more than an adjunct of mathematics. There were no more lessons on the history of chemistry, classes became just the taking of notes as dictated by the teacher; I attempted to translate the alien tongue in which he droned, but could only write any old thing to fill the book up, keeping five-bar gates that recorded how often he used his pet sayings, falling behind ever faster, understanding nothing. The work involved fewer and fewer physical experiments and more and more calculations, formulae, dense terminology, figures, figures, maths, maths, maths. Physics had lost its promise too; I missed the point, lost my way, and again all I heard were demands for calculations, figures, graphs, maths, maths, maths.

So I was innumerate and inept. With some relief, I dropped biology and physics at the end of my third year, and at the age of sixteen my final abject retreat was my withdrawal from chemistry lessons after a dire mock 'O' Level exam (Ungraded) to cram in an attempt to rescue my Maths 'O' level.

These days it's truer than ever that someone not scientifically literate is at a disadvantage, not just in understanding the world (or the universe, come to that) but in fighting against the darkness that always looms. For one thing, I would like to be able to tell the difference between true science and the TV adverts that blabber about wonder products, beta lampoonins, procozymones or whatever miracle ingredient they are hyping to blind their audience with—gulp—science.

We are beset with pseudoscience, anti-science and storms of dubious statistics; owing to my failure to release my inner scienteest, I possess insufficient coherent arguments to combat their dubious, half-baked claims. I am forever arguing on the backfoot, nervous and at a disadvantage, looking for someone cleverer to rise up to the fight.

What, apart from me working harder and perhaps asking for help (I never thought of that) could have remedied the problem? It strikes me now that apart from those short lessons on Lavoisier et al., we were never taught the context, the *point* of science—indeed, we were never taught the *point* of anything. Our lessons were tasks we were obliged to undertake, why waste time on explanations? An exposition on the scientific method, on how to think critically, how to test a theory—now wouldn't *that* have helped? I could at least have learned to think, rather than just look, like a bit of a boffin.

That, then, was my short, doomed career as a scienteest. From Aristotle to Einstein, I had the chance to stand on the shoulders of giants:

I fell off.

Promissory

At eighteen, I had never seen so much money. Not cash, but figures on a cool blue slip made out in my name: it had to last three months, but still it seemed huge. It was mine to manage, alone. What if I proved as inept with real money as I had with schoolbook exercises? (If A is given three months' grant money and he then passes Record Shop B and Pub C, at what point will L subtend to zero?) The figures went to my head for a minute, but I was sobered by the still air of the banking hall; this was a place of business, of sensible decision-making, where clear-headed, responsible adults come to pay in, draw out; no childishness or reckless spendthriftery here.

That hall reminded me of the Ironmarket Bank, where my father used to deposit his cheques, draw his cash: it was the most imposing space I had seen—hushed, peaceful, orderly. Nobody there would raise their voice or disrupt the stillness; nobody would dare.

It was portentous, self-assured, safe. The past lodged there, nurturing, nest-egging, the future in calm, monied harmony. The doors were solid, dark wood, the walls wood-panelled, the windows half-white so that light could enter but idle gazes could not. The floors were cold, hard, self-important; steps echoed long and deeply resonant. Pens were thin-chain fixed to holders on small chest-height desks, and on narrow shelves on the wall; they were ballpoints, yet they exuded a quill-pen air. The staff sat behind old-fashioned desks were divided from the rest of the world by clean, clear glass. The place should have been cold, unfriendly, especially to a child, but its atmosphere was dignified, semi-distant yet benevolent.

A cheque in my name; a paying-in slip. I queued to await the attention of a cool-glass banker. I was using an account, paying bills, joining the grown-up world. It was telling that this was my first visit to a building on the campus; not the Faculty or any other academic building, not even the Student Union. It all began, stemmed from, here. The cheque, the slip, the queuing, it was the process of admission to academe, handing in my tickets, going through the gates and into the future. Money and studies; it was up to me now. Work hard, get that degree and it's another visa in your hand—show that paperwork, doors will open, jobs, jobs, jobs, jobs. They will want you and your degree, and you will shimmy past queues of spotty ex-schoolkids with no qualifications or hope. The degree was the promissory note of the highest value, my initiation into the transactional nature of life.

My reasons for going to university should have been pure—love of study, adoration of books, the desire above all to improve my mind, but the present and near-future leaned in, darkening the way ahead; the school leavers were walking straight to a different sort of queue—the dole. Tuck yourself away for three years and things will get better, there will be more jobs and that certificate will be more valuable than ever. In years prior, a man with a degree could go from job to job, cherrypicking; he could quit, travel a while, then pick up again with ease, enjoying himself for a time, then developing a career and, like a cat, having prowled, grow domesticated, settled, satisfied. The same ease would beckon me, the clouds would pass. 'University!' bellowed Big Jace confidentially, 'If you get to Uni, you're in the top ten per cent in the country! *Top ten!*' I was safe with tens, I could work with them—percentages less so, but figuring ten out of one hundred wasn't too difficult even for me. An elite, the entitled, the well-paid. All right, the not-yet well-paid, but the anointed.

Three of four windows were open; there were many people, a multitude of promissory notes, but the fourth window remained closed. Why was that so, when so many waited to make their compact with the future? *I promise if you bank my cheque I shall work hard, please my professors, pass my exams, redeem your investment in the future. I promise; I do. My word, as one of the ten percent.* My uncle certainly did not regard the promissory as any sort of investment. He berated me for living on an 'unearned income', which, as far as he could see, was coming out of his wage packet, just as he was paying 'for all the idlers down the dole'. I argued back. We got nowhere.

It *was* a question of the future: years before, my great-grandfather was a railwayman. He went into the industry as a young man, spent his working life there, no question or conception of walking away, of experimenting, toying with something new, opting for a quick tour around the world. He was devoted to his trade, there was an understanding, a bond of honour between worker and worked-for, and his employers never betrayed him or let him down. They knew better than to lose a good man, and that he was no lackey, unafraid to air a grievance or support a workmate.

Time moved, and something changed, something fundamental, detrimental. Like great-grandad, my uncle was devoted to his job, experienced and respected by peers, but that bond, though still purported, was no longer honoured. Motor Traction lost interest in the business of transporting workers, shoppers, schoolchildren, to and fro; their passengers were now, like their employees, mobile counters in an economic board game, 'Beggar My Rival'.

My uncle was taken off his beloved buses, and with other senior staff deposited on unfriendly roadsides to watch, time and take notes of rival services, allowing MT to assess what to avoid, to exploit, and then match those services, steal passengers, dish the competition. Having done this, MT would reduce their unrivalled services, or cut them altogether. The new times, the new way; don't just beggar your rivals—cut their throats. And the message to the unhappy workforce? 'Argue and you're out—there's plenty as'll take your job.'

I would be nobody's pawn: that was how the promissory would pay off.

At twenty-one, I left university with an overdraft of £100—quite a lot of debt then. It was paid off by a real adult, one who didn't scold or criticise, who was sensitive, pragmatic, who had once banked in that cool, wood-panelled hall. It wasn't paid at the Ironmarket Bank, for that was gone, taken over then closed-down-not-needed; everyone was cutting, cut-throating now. I felt a curious nostalgia for those cool halls, but that was hardly at the forefront of my mind, for my plan had failed.

Things had not improved while I tucked myself away a-studying. I would not be ten-percenting. Far from it. I would be back before a counter with a glass screen and a piece of paper in hand, a parsimonious pledge of money, but ominously silent on the once-rich promise of the future.

An Afternoon Out

The window was down, and my hair slipstreamed wildly, whipping the faces of the two lads sitting in the back seat with me as the car sped into the summer breeze. Monkey was driving and I could imagine but couldn't see his grin as he heard the two boys yelping at the sharp stings from the lashing tips of my wild locks. Monkey's girlfriend had given me one of her hair grips to provide some control, but it was in the pocket of my waistcoat as a memento, a small treasure. Monkey had reason to be pleased about the situation and so did I; not the same reason, though, not quite. Monks had a bit of a funny-bone for people suffering pain (not too-serious pain, I mean a sort of sharpened sense of slapstick), but he had another reason too, I was going to call it secret but it wasn't that; unspoken, yes, that's better.

Durber, his girlfriend, didn't react, she just looked straight ahead at the tall country hedgerows as they came at us then raced by. We weren't heading anywhere in particular, and the vortex of wind and whipcord hair seemed the whole point, certainly the high point, of the trip from where Monkey sat. Durber's real name was Tessa Villiers; it was my doing, I needed to hide my fondness for her beneath a lit-wit nickname and somehow it had stuck. She wasn't fooled but Monkey seemed to be—that or he didn't care. Monkey seemed able to forget for long periods that she even existed, sometimes when she was right there with him, but he loved her sort-of. A close second to his car, maybe. But his negligence didn't stand in the way of his secret wishing.

Perry and Rob, the lads under the lash in the back seat with me, cried out good-naturedly for Durber to close the windows, but Monkey had sole access to the controls, and he affected deafness as they suffered in the wind-tunnel. For a moment I wished I'd had those beads put in my locks, just as I'd boasted I would, strings of beads that would have nine-tailed them good and proper, or fishhooks, even better, fishhooks, barbs, something to catch at them, tear, draw blood. That cruel moment ended, come and gone again in an instant like a child's tantrum, and none of them knew of it.

'Shall we stop for lunch at a pub?' Durber half-turned her head and let the breeze swish her words to the back of the car.

Rob and Perry assented eagerly, and Monkey slowed us down, reluctantly beginning the search. He was driving, he had no interest in beer; the one thing that put him off drink. Durber was trying to be kind, she knew I liked a beer, it was a hot day, but unwittingly she was doing me no favours. She wanted to rescue Perry and Rob, obviously, she was being kind all round. But I didn't want to stop and nor did Monkey. I liked these two men, truly I did, and yet I owed them a little suffering.

We rolled onto the gravel drive of a country pub and pulled in on the small car park. Perry eyed me with suspicion, as if I had planned what he had just been through. Rob was laughing as if it were a merry prank played on someone else. Durber scolded me about the hair band, I made a pantomime search of my pockets and produced it. She chuckled and stepped into the bar, and I, once again, pocketed the band. I held the door for Monkey, and he gave me a wicked, conspiratorial look. I stepped into the pub last, wishing I was not there at all. I was trying to control my racing mind as I worked on a strategy.

'Thanks no, I'll get my own,' was on the tip of my tongue, ready for panicked blurting. Luckily, Monkey had barrelled up to the bar ahead of all comers, one of his finest qualities, and I relaxed, I could just have the one, make it last, pay him back later. It only remained to pretend not to want any lunch.

Drinks in hand, we strolled back into the beautiful sunshine, to the beer garden; Durber sat, her skirt caught on the edge of the rough wooden table and she hung suspended for a moment, awaiting rescue; this came from Perry, who offered a gentle steadying hand as she freed herself, then released his grip lingeringly as she settled herself and smiled her thanks. Monkey was last out of the bar and he had Durber's drink as well as his own, there was no way he could help. The look he gave Perry was a witherer. There was a crack in Monkey's easy attitude towards Durber, and Perry was it; Perry had helped her to that seat with the same hand that one-time had placed a ring on her finger, in an engagement that was more to do with compatible families than compatible people and didn't survive her first term at university, but Monks knew about it and did not like it. He was wary of Rob too; Rob's family owned the pub we were at; I got the idea that they owned half the county too. Monkey feared that Perry could lure her with the past, and Rob could lure her with lucre. It didn't show a flattering opinion of Durber but demonstrated that even the most relaxed and friendly man I had ever known could be tortured by his anxieties.

Though Rob and Perry had been easy, charming and friendly with me at the party the night before, the conversation was difficult.

'What do you do?' asked Perry. It was just chat, as he had clearly been trained to perform easily with all types; he truly didn't know what a hand-grenade he was lobbing to me. I made a clumsy mime of plying a pen.

'You're a writer?' Rob blinked, impressed.

'He means he's signing on.' Monkey was quick to get that in, he was a good friend but then again just occasionally a lousy one, as it sank in slowly to me that to these young men my code-mime meant nothing. They evinced polite disbelief that someone could be without work—this from men whose jobs came from daddy, like pocket money or toys.

'Perhaps you'd have more luck if you had a—er—'

'Haircut' was the word Rob left dangling.

'Any employer who hires on the basis of hairstyles is an idiot,' I declared passionately.

'Well Rob's dad wouldn—' it was Perry's turn to be a bad friend and leave his words hanging over a chasm.

'There are no jobs out there anyway,' I said sulkily. 'Hair or no hair.' I meant the last bit as a get-back at Monkey; like me he'd dodged the barber throughout university, but he'd had his thinning locks cut back to look good for graduation, and then to please stupid, shallow bosses. I'd suffered the same conversation with Durber's mum, but she lacked the lads' friendliness and goodwill. She knew a ne'er do well when she saw one; she despised me and had no compunction about letting me know it. For the frostbite reception, also for want of originality or because I couldn't be bothered to waste time crafting her a better one, I gave her the nickname Ice Dragon. 'The split ends alone would put anyone off...' I heard her confide foghorn-style to another guest. The only good thing about my encounter with her was that it made her fonder of Monkey—a relative matter, he was a parvenu, no good for her daughter, but she now knew Durber could do worse.

Durber had ordered chips with her sandwich, and she let me share those; fact is I got most of them, she'd done it deliberately: she knew. It had cost me nearly half a week's money to get to that party—and hours on the train. I must have been insane to do it, I was really going to struggle when I got home. I was terrified to spend another ten pence. But here I was in the company of people whose veins pulsed with liquid cash, and who would doubtless have spent the equivalent of my week's dole on a single meal out without the least worry.

Durber, protective and aware, presided over that lunch, she took charge; if Rob or Perry started any talk that smelt faintly of money, she touched the tiller and steered us away, and if Monkey started drooling after one of the expensive, shimmering things in that car park, she quietened him and changed the subject. Rob and Perry grew fond of the idea of another drink, but she scotched that one, ostensibly for Monkey's sake as he shouldn't have to look at others swigging beer while he was on softs, and it was decided we would set off again.

There was not a scintilla of spite in Perry or Rob, just otherworldly bemusement that someone could have no job or money, that such a thing was possible. I felt I was under glass and curious gazes, but not with malice. But there had been malicious ears at the party, and above the gossipy hubbub I caught meant-to-be-heard asides from guests, spurred by the Dragon; *'Dole!'*, *'Not earning!'* Everyone became protective of the food on their plates, as if I would snatch it in feral frenzy, and nobody but Monks and Durber offered me a drink.

'Have you tried—' Perry had begun to advise; but his tongue began to twist.

'Yes, he has.' Durber was firm, and Perry was grateful to curtail his faltering attempt. But the whispering went on; *'Unemployed!'*; *'That hair! No wonder.'*

'We'll avoid the hair-storm this time.' Durber laid the law down to Monkey and me as we gathered around the car. Letting Perry into the passenger seat,

Monkey rearranged the rest of us in the back, Rob first, then me, then Durber. Satisfied, Monkey took his seat and we set back off. Durber made me wear the hairband and told Monks to keep the windows open just a crack this time.

Pushed in close to her, I imagined that I was the driver of an open-topped car and that it was only us, my left arm draped around her shoulders and our hair flying wild in the carefree summer air. Then I recalled I would need both hands to steer on those winding, dangerous country roads. And I couldn't afford a car. Nor could I afford daydreams.

Giro

Woolsend Post Office was in a row of terraced houses on a road called the Vale, a busy shopping street and a world to itself until the supermarket expansion of the 1970s and the cold winds of the 80s began its slow but unstoppable downfall. It was set back from the road, like its neighbours, but unlike them had no front wall, no gate: only a pillar box standing in what would have been the garden.

You stepped into a pen-and-paper, inkpad smell, and displays of greeting cards, ruled notebooks with bright red covers imploring 'write in me', local notices, and small ads. Not much else, as you were in the front room of a small house. It was made more cramped by the counters, with scales for parcels. Behind glass windows two slow-moving, eccentric owners dished out stamps, issued or cashed Postal Orders, took in large packets, and talked at friendly leisure with queuing pensioners.

As a youngster I collected my Nan's pension for her as she couldn't make it to the Vale. Every week I would shrink back in terror of being accused and detained as a fraud and thief, because in place of my full name and address on the section marked 'I give permission to collect my pension to [full name and address here]', she put 'My Grandson'. By this time, the Vale was a shadow of itself; no longer did everyone know everyone and their business: but the old ways were not dead yet, the couple behind the counter knew whose grandson I was; *shuffle-inkpad-stamp-shuffle* and every week I took the money down the hill and paid it over.

I was away at university three years, returning in the summer of 1984. Nan was gone and the Vale had faded still further, but the Post Office and its odd, quietly intimidating couple was still in business. I stood in the queue again, but this time my slip of green paper was the giro for my payments of Supplementary Benefit. This time the feeling of lurking guilt prickled harder, more deeply, with every *shuffle-inkpad-stamp-shuffle*. They knew who I was, that wasn't the problem: suspicion surrounded the giro-holder like a miasma; why are you here, why are you cashing this, why aren't you working? Suspicion and hostility: the miners had begun their strike that Spring, and the divisions were becoming clearer.

The government had decided that the unemployed, the miners, anyone who gave them sympathy or support, was the enemy within. Why don't you get a job? Why, when no one is working there, don't you get a job at the pit? Why? Why? Why not? *Shuffle-inkpad-stamp-shuffle*. Green slips convert into money, but slowly, reluctantly; the powers that be think you did enough to look for work—but we don't. Un-earned income.

Every giro day I felt this silent, questioning

resentment, not just from the blank faces behind the counter's glass, but the queueing pensioners. It was like facing the Ice Dragon again; justify yourself; no, don't bother, your case is hopeless.

Why are you collecting a giro? Why aren't you working?

I'm as confused as you are. I hid from the storm for three years, I came out with this piece of paper that was supposed to be my passport to well-paid work, my ticket to the future: but it's just a piece of paper to most people. To employers it says 'Overqualified'; 'Don't take him on, he will get a better job and leave'. Mostly it's 'We'll get back to you'; but they don't. Most don't even reply to the letters, forms or calls.

You should go from place to place looking for work.

Yeah, they love that. Really. It works so well.

You have less right to be sarcastic than you have to that money you're drawing. You could get a job if you wanted to.

Do you remember how this government got into power? There were a million people on the dole, they said it was a tragedy, that it was the fault of the then-government, that everything would be fixed if we voted for them. Even my Mum bought that promise. Now it's five years later, unemployment is three million and more, they still say it's a 'tragedy', but now the story is that it's the fault of feckless shirkers who don't want work. Isn't that narrative a little suspect? They either had no magic solution—in which case they were lying—or they've shelved it because they prefer things this way, which makes them something else entirely. Makes you think, eh?

No.

I feared as much.

Get a job at Raston's. There's always jobs at Raston's. It's been here for over a hundred years.

It's closing, didn't you hear? Look, things have changed, I like it no more than you do. Do you know, I attended a 'Restart' interview at the dole the other day? Ironic, as I haven't even been able to 'start', but there you have it. The interviewer was slightly surprised and grateful I even showed up. 'I've looked through your notes. Let's be straight, there isn't much we can do to help, not at the moment. By the way, I liked your answer to: 'Are there any other barriers to your finding employment.'

I had put 'Margaret Thatcher'.

You're just enjoying living off our backs

That was unfair. Nobody—and there were plenty of us in our small town—enjoyed being on the dole, no matter how much some of the tabloids flogged that line. The only exceptions were Ben the Poet and Big Jace, for their own reasons. The subsistence income allowed Ben, in his flat above a greengrocer's shop, to embrace the artist-garret cliché with fervour, living off dreams, unconsummated schemes. His poetry was of a very abstract sort, in that he never wrote any; in some inexplicable way, perhaps ambling the street one day, he would be recognised as an unsung genius and elevated to star-poet status. All by someone who could read his aura, perhaps, as there was nothing else to read. Jace was more practical; a self-taught guitarist, he was gigging on the pub circuit with a 50s-60s combo, The Time Wasters. Good fun they were too, though their Johnny

B Goode outlasted many prog rock albums. Jace, who had vowed self-destruction should he not become a major star by his twenty-fifth, found his dole useful as petrol money. I assume he never said anything of this to the Restart people.

Invited to Jace's one afternoon to hear him work out ideas on a new guitar, I heard a 'come-in' and I stepped from bright sunlight into a confusing contrast of darkness and dazzle, which stopped me as I entered the living room. The curtains were closed but for slits, little was visible other than that stark sight of a hard-backed chair with a small table next to it, on which stood an angle-poise lamp, poised low, which cut a cone of light around the chair and deepened the shadows beyond.

'Jason's busy,' said a chair opposite the light-cone. I claim credit for not swearing in surprise. 'But he thought you might profit from a word with me.'

The man in the chair had got used to the light-and-dark; he could see me; I could still not make him out. It was just a big armchair overspilled with shadow.

'Sit down young fella, sit down, I won't bite.' I trudged to the spotlit chair and did as asked. I had fallen into a trap and there was no way out: I was in the lair of William The Wise, Jace's dad, whose chief occupation these days was dispensing pearls from The Wisdom Chair. I had encountered him before but was rescued by Jace bursting in to tell me to get a move on, we were due to sign on. This time, however, I had no excuse, no get-out.

Where the hell was bloody Jace?

'Jason tells me you are struggling to secure a job.' The Wise began mildly.

'Well, yes, we all are…'

'It's a shame to see good lads idle when there's work going begging. I believe I can help. You'll see there's a notepad and pen on the table next to you; they're not there by accident.'

Oh boy, did I want a word with Jace about this set-up.

'These are difficult times, there's no denying it, but with sufficient application a promising young man can find a suitable role.' The voice from The Wisdom Chair rose to its purpose.

Where the hell was bloody Jace?

I was tempted to pick up the notepad and doodle, but it wasn't beyond the man to demand to see my work afterwards, to make sure I'd been paying attention. Instead, I made rapid scribbles in my normal handwriting, which is joyfully illegible. Mainly, they read *bollocksbollocksbollocksbollockbollocks*. William's wisdom lacked the frosty bite of the Ice Dragon, instead pitching closer to the well-meant but chiefly irrelevant, outdated, redundant offerings of everyone else, including Restart, but with a much greater self-certitude.

'Jason is in the garage, restringing his amplifier or something.' That was my dismissal. Jace lurked in semi-dark too, concentrating on strumming so he didn't have to look up at me. I hoped he knew the sort of review his new songs were now going to get.

Why don't you go down South? That's where the jobs are.

My family, my friends are all here. Why should I uproot? Besides, if I leave that's one more youngster gone from here, probably never to return. One more wage (eventually) that won't get spent here; one more young family (oh, eventually) that won't balance out the ageing population or pay taxes that help everyone else—paying your pensions, for instance.

Are you calling us old?

That wasn't my point. I can't bloody win, can I?

Language! Why don't you walk down to Webster's Mill, they're always taking on. Fix you up in a jiffy, they will.

It occurred to me that there was a strong resemblance between Webster's Mill and Michelle Ockendon, late of my A Level English class. Specifically, the look of frozen horror as, writhing with embarrassed self-consciousness, I approached them to ask an important question. Also, come to think of it, the 'I'll let you know' from each, for which I am still waiting, and presumably will continue to do so.

I was down the pit at your age. Why don't you get a job at the pit?

There's a strike on, it would be wrong even if I could. And if the miners don't win, there will be no more pits, haven't you read the papers? The government says the pits are 'uneconomic'. And, as a sidelight, don't you think the government's been dishonest? They swore there was no pit closure programme, that they hadn't appointed a hatchet-man to force the process through. Now they've appointed that hatchet-man and the pits will close. More young men, older men, family men, lining up for their giros.

It won't happen. They promised it wouldn't.

Watch and wait.

Your poor parents!

Agreed, they're worried sick. And they're all that stands between me and complete misery.

They should throw you out, make you stand on your own two feet.

Cheers for that.

Shuffle-inkpad-stamp-shuffle. Take money, head down, slink out, breathe in pen-paper-ink smell but look up not at all, catch no eyes. This isn't the future you were expecting. Tough luck, sunbeam.

Woolsend PO is gone now; there is no pillar box; the nearest box is half a mile; the nearest Post Office much further than that. The little terraced house has a wrought-iron gate and a low garden wall. Woolsend pit is gone, as are Nightingale, Hepworth, Decken, Goldenway, all its quondam neighbours. I did voluntary work for a while, learned to advise on the benefits system and help people to deal with debts. But there were no jobs in that field, except you-know-where. So yes, I ended up going down South. Where the work was.

Always Keep The Receipt

'Things are looking up,' Big Jace pronounced, using his empty glass as an echo-chamber. 'At least these days we're all in work.'

This did not receive the rousing *yeahyeahyeahs* and clash of raised glasses Jace expected, and his surprise was plain. Jace was always optimistic; seven pints had made him more so, but he was not usually insanely optimistic until at least his eleventh.

'Well... we are, aren't we?'

'Working, but not necessarily in a job,' cavilled Ben the Poet, who was on a compulsory government scheme that involved returning a randomised card index to some semblance of order; the index was redundant, replaced by a computer, but he and his 'team' ploughed on, for a quiet life and a ten-quid top up on their benefits. 'And my "job" has got a big nose, big ears and a tail, and first appeared in "Steamboat Willie" in 1928.'

Jace gawped.

'And is married to Minnie,' Ben felt he needed to add.

Jace turned to me. 'And yours?'

'Is so good I wish it *was* a job. But the funding runs

out soon, so I either carry on as a volunteer, or deck the whole thing.'

'At least it's helping you gain skills, get another job.'

'It isn't a job,' interjected Ben stubbornly.

'I've got a degree, Jace. A bloody *degree*. "Skills". Top ten percent, remember that? Still no job.' My mind drifted back to the days of the Promissory. Look how that shook out.

My non-job job was at Decken Advice Project. I was convinced I'd blown the interview. I was told that the job involved helping people claim their statutory rights; I brain-froze and was forced to ask in a squeak what 'statutory' meant; that did not feel good. But my luck held, and although it was a government scheme it was a good one. I enjoyed it and, yes, though I hate to say Jace was right, I gained something. No, I gained a great deal.

With no money of my own with which to be a consumer, I had to advise other consumers on those statutory rights and how to enforce them; the sale of goods; the supply of goods and services; offer, acceptance and consideration; does the buyer have capacity to contract; good title (does the seller *actually* own the goods they purport to sell? The buyer of my mate's car, stolen while we were at a concert, learned something on the last of those subjects). And I learned one should never buy a car privately—just never. Your rights and redress? None, pretty much. *Caveat emptor.* Caveat Everybody, as it turned out.

Decken drowsed in post-industrial dreams, restlessly

awaiting an ever-postponed reawakening. A railway line ran through the town, elevated, overhead, casting shadows on the streets. The pit was closed, the site a fenced-off tip; its spoil heaps dirty foothills on the edge of town, no longer growing, settling into disuse. When snow fell, they looked like a range of giant, absurd Christmas puddings. The tombstone of Decken's other dead-and-gone (cut and run, rather) major employer was a large, empty factory, a giant of pale, ruined brick, scarred with spray-paint, broken-paned. Time and progress could be counted off by the number of new broken windows—the future, flung stone by stone. This place would crumble and fall before there was a sniff of any plan to revive and reopen it. A government minister called by one day, whistle-stop, talking of 'regeneration'; by nightfall, he was gone, never to return, and so were more windows.

Some towns, communities, had been drawn into decline, sucked into a spiral by forces few understood but which were represented to them as inexorable elementals, nature admirable in its cold, undiscriminating brutality. Decken, however, had been invited, inveigled. Its pitmen had been persuaded that their deep mine would not close if only they broke their strike and went back down; once on the dole they had been persuaded that, with the prevalence of pneumoconiosis and its ilk, they should be on sickness benefits, which helped ease the unemployment statistics but not their pockets. They would later be castigated by the same government as workshy malingerers.

The day and night shifts at the red-brick factory had been given short notice, short payoffs, short shrift. They were promised a golden future jobsjobsjobs, if they would just *go*. People in work envied those on the dole because they thought they had it easy; those on the dole envied those on the sick, because they were paid a little more. Those who had not-much were encouraged to be jealous of those who had little; those who had little were encouraged to loathe those who had nothing. There was a green-eyed hierarchy; everyone thought their neighbour had *more* and didn't deserve it. It was difficult to resist the feeling that all this was part of a plan; the decline of Decken had been judged a price worth paying.

I was greeted on my first day by McLennan, the Project's deputy manager. Small—five foot six if trying hard—sandy haired, friendly, firm of handshake; his face lined, but every line the track of old, deep, warm smiles. I had to keep asking him what he'd said, as he spoke in a quick, deep Dundonian accent.

It turned out the first thing he said was, 'Ah, you're the laddie who didn't know what "statutory" meant. Pillock!' I liked him at once. 'You'll get used to it,' he counselled of his accent. 'It's how I win my benefit appeals. The sassenachs don't understand me, so they think I must be right!'

It was from McLennan I learned what I needed to know about benefit law and debt advice; but, crucially, he taught me how to fight and not give up. 'Three rules,' he pronounced: 'Always keep the receipt; if they sell you a dud, sue em; and for benefits—always appeal.'

He was a master at those appeals—hard work, research and voluminous knowledge won the day, not an impenetrable accent. And he was a sharp negotiator too, though he claimed to favour more unconventional methods of dispute resolution. When I was embroiled in an unending argument with a rogue trader, McLennan's prescription was the judicious application of 'a brick wrapped up in a sock.' When the Department for Health and Social Security made and clung to ridiculous decisions, he said, 'Away and get yer coat—we'll go to their office an break all the windehs.'

The manager of our Project tutted at such talk, but one day, after a draining, deadlock call with the DHSS, she emerged from her office shouting 'McLennan! Assemble the window-breakers!' Without McLennan's presence, support, and indomitable spirit, I may never have thrived in the job, I may have lost energy and heart, shied away, let the fight go out of me, but he would never allow such a thing. I have not seen him in over thirty years, but his influence remains, including a habit of saying *'Och, away!'* when annoyed. It sounds all wrong in an English Midlands accent, but it has become reflexive.

Over my months at Decken, I learned not only how broke many of the people were there, but how in this old coal town, stripped of mines, there were still means of extraction. It was astonishing to watch the money-miners batten and feed, rich pickings from the poor:

you take a small amount each time, but if you take it from thousands of people, that's them pocket-picked and you minted. They'll not miss what they never had. I was astonished at how many shady operators were out there, waiting to sell dubious white goods or cardboard furniture at inflated prices, plus how many even shadier finance houses hovered in the gloom, offering 'easy' credit at sky-high percentage rates to help with the process.

Many people in Decken were on Supplementary Benefit, and at that time they could get grants, 'single payments', for essential items they couldn't afford: they were quickly relieved of these in exchange for fall-apart goods. Nowadays the same happens, but the money is a loan, so they lose out twice. The cooperative parasites swam in the blood of the community and were the only ones to wax fat.

'We provide a public service. We regard ourselves as friends of the family,' remarked one moneylender to me in response to a complaint that his debt collector had hammered on one broke family's door at midnight, yelling that they were 'no better than thieves'. The commonest sight in town was debt collectors scurrying door to door, in haste to get there ahead of the rent man.

Newly privatised gas and electricity firms sent teams of eager young people onto the streets to 'survey' members of the public, asking passers-by a set of questions and then, with a charming smile, if they might sign and date this page here as proof that they were surveyed? Well, thought the mark, that charming young person might not get their pay if they can't prove they did the work. It would be about a week later when the mark received a letter thanking them for signing a contract to switch energy suppliers, *you have been tricked and we hope you will be happy with us in future.*

If you were in debt with them, as many in Decken were, you could expect, if you did not have one already, a coin meter to be fitted, recovering a dollop of debt for every 50p that clacked into the slot. If you ran out of 50ps you were cut off, but you'd done it to yourself, hadn't you? Peel away their elaborate promises of 'considerate customer service' in their adverts and PR blurb, the reality came home.

'We're not accepting excuses—we're going in hard,' one charmer told me as I telephoned his company to protest its treatment of a pensioner couple bedevilled by perished pensions and perishing cold. Not only was the company going to cut off the gas, but they were also proposing to bill the couple's son, who came in every day to look after them, as the 'beneficial user' of the fuel in the home. They didn't want to hear any arguments that this was cruel, crazy, unlawful, immoral; he enjoyed the heat and light just as much as did the old folks, yeah? Well then. They were going in hard.

'They'll be chargin us for drawin breath next!' remarked the bemused old miner.

'Bloody ell, dunner givvem ideas!' cried his wife, muttering as an addendum, 'Much gets more, bloody ell…'

Even the TVs had slots: when people were in debt, their creditors raged against them having the luxury of television, but as a countervailing force, a plethora of firms really, really did want them to view, view, view the screens—hour upon hour, coin after coin—so they got to push their products. People were at home, without jobs, why exclude them from the bonanza?

Even TV-ad names on the depleted high street could stun, with stated after-sales policies (stated over the phone of course, not in writing) such as, 'Once it's out of our door, it's not our problem anymore'. The significance of the statutory certainly sank in: customers were bamboozled into signing screeds of small print assuring them, *This does not affect your statutory rights'* while, line by line, removing, extirpating, them all.

Other clever operators dreamed up complicated and costly 'extended guarantees' that purported to *add* to consumers' rights in law, but were so riddled with exclusions they were of no use to anyone—a close cousin of this scheme raised its head a little later in the form of 'payment protection' policies pretending to provide a haven in the event of unemployment, sold with relentless, oleaginous dishonesty, as anyone who became unemployed was automatically excluded from benefiting from the cover. The message to the denizens of Decken was clear: you are clinging to the margins of normal life, but for that you must pay-pay-pay.

'I know my rights!' people would insist staunchly; McLennan said they were usually quoting either 'common knowledge' that was surely common but not real knowledge, or legal tips from brokespine books, forty years out of date. To be sure, there *were* rights—for instance for your goods to be of merchantable quality, as described and fit for their purpose. There was the right to a refund, but people were frequently diverted into the cul-de-sac of a credit note, trapping them with the very vendor with whom a trusting trade relationship had just collapsed. The credit note was a poisoned promissory, a dud, devalued currency, a memo reading 'your pocket has just been picked'. You needed to keep your receipt, but with some traders you may as well have waved a used bus ticket. Even for those who truly knew their rights; how to secure them? That took time, pen on paper, command of words, determination, self-confidence, but, moreover, money. Court fees, lawyers' fees—or argue your case, tongue-tied and uncertain.

There were laws against the imposition of extortionate credit terms, but the lenders were safe, the laws unenforceable: legal costs, a popular anathema for mathematics that may prevent people from ever knowing how they were being cheated. And for those who fought? Pay, pay, pay first; justice later.

A purveyor of posh furniture dreamed up a handy side-line wrinkle; in the attic of their shop, they opened a cut-price section called 'Rummages', where chairs and sofas were piled high and sold cheap, a bargain basement elevated to the rafters. Naturally this attracted skint bargain-hunters, and trouble was inevitable. Complaint after complaint about

Rummages arrived at the office. Our visiting consumer affairs expert was Annette. At thirty she looked as youthful as a new graduate learning her first job, but she was knowledgeable, experienced, self-assured, cool, professional and impressive—not least to me. She carried off catwalk looks and trim elegance while crushing with cheerful ruthlessness any attempt to little-woman her. I fought feebly against the rising of feelings first encountered in A Level English and later in a small car speeding through country lanes.

McLennan knew: 'Soon as you get any problems, you can't wait to grab that phone—"*Annneeeeettttteee!*"'

As part of my training, I accompanied Annette on home visits, the better to inspect large items of allegedly faulty goods, size up the prospects of negotiations with the vendors and possible redress. We set off to a small council estate to inspect a settee, late Rummages. The aggrieved consumer had already written to the shop manager and having seen his reply—headed 'Your Ref: SC/UM'—we were not optimistic.

We pulled up at a small end-terrace with scaffolding as its front wall's last desperate hope and an over-large front window that looked as tenuous and rainbow-shot as a soap bubble. Indoors was a scenario of frayed carpets and old furniture. The place was clean, but bare and unostentatious, there had been no money coming in here for many a year, and old, loved trinkets clung together for safety on a scarred sideboard, reluctant to go down the road 'to my uncle's', to keep the wolf from the warped and rainwashed door.

The tenants were elderly and clearly not enjoying good health; the man, white-haired, sunken-cheeked and uneasy of breathing, rested his chin on the rounded handle of his walking stick as he sat in an attempt at upright in an unforgiving tall wooden chair by the window; I guessed he had been cleared off his habitual haven, the settee, so we could inspect it. Already I could see tears, rents in the back of the thing ('Opened up two seconds after they delivered it,' huffed the aggrieved purchaser, her husband nodding as she gesticulated, as if he were being conducted) and the covering was coming away from the arms and the sides. Annette looked closely and took some quick, crabbed notes.

'But that's not even the worst of it,' the complainant continued, sitting us down with you-there, you-there gestures; I braced for the impact of a sharp spring or a jutting piece of jagged wood, but as a matter of fact the thing felt quite comfortable, 'Every time I sit, given a few minutes, I feel all wrong, as if there's something... I *itch*.' Annette shot to her feet, making her own gesture to me, *up, up!* The penny was horribly slow to drop, but I sprang to her side.

'Well, I think we have sufficient information for now.' Annette was smooth, diplomatic. 'I'll contact the shop and hear what they have to say. I'll be in touch.'

We left as quickly as we could, but not before the old man rose from his chair, desperate to return to his haven, only to lurch, stagger, fall backwards and put his walking-stick through the window; the bubble burst in triangle shards.

'Ahhh, look what you've done now, you stupid old man!' scolded his wife as we fled.

Annette's charm didn't soothe the manager of Rummages; he expressed his immunity in rising indignation that was plain even over a muffled-tinny phone line. 'These people can't expect top quality. They should get the idea from the name—eh?'

'They can, though, expect goods to be worth the money they paid and not to start falling apart the moment they get them home.'

'At those prices they get what they're given.'

Annette gave up on charm. In the background, McLennan mimed the brick-sock; she ignored him, however tempted, and pressed on.

'Whatever the price, they have rights to goods of a decent standard. And ones that aren't chockful of fleas.'

'*My* furniture is *not* full of fleas! They're on Mace Mill Estate, *that's* where the fleas come from, it's where they were bloody invented!'

'Are you prepared to refund their money?'

'They can ave a credit note if it'll shut em up.'

'Their right in law is—'

'I don't want the law, I want *justice*!' Mr Rummage was impugned, incandescent; Annette remained calm, polite, unperturbed. She got the money back, 'To get shut of yer all!' and we wondered if the settee would end up back in the pile at the top of the shop.

For those who had a little money, there were pilot fish

and sharks. The customer would go on holiday, and there in the cobbled streets of their cove-heaven were the pilot fish; aren't the houses lovely around here, have you seen these apartments by the beach, why they are time-shares, you plainly love this little hideaway, just think, you could have a stake in one of these, holiday any time you want, live the dream. Come to our presentation tonight, no obligation! And so to the sharks: *nopressurenopressure nopressurenopressure nopressurenopressure nopressurenopressure*, they held on to their prey with smarm and charm and tricks and traps.

How can I leave, I may offend this lovely person here, and all he wants to do is for me to sign here, give my bank details here? They ring a bell every time someone signs and everyone stands up, applauds and cheers; I want the bell to ring for me, I want everyone on their feet clamouring for me, let me sign, let me sign. Ogod I've signed—dingdong—and I didn't want to - dingdong—is there any way out of this?

Or:

Into your home came the beaming rep bearing the Kayway Cleaner: they would obligingly demonstrate its superior functioning by passing it over a swipe of your living room, creating a sanitised streak, making the rest look dowdy and you a bad housekeeper. Impressed, you would ask how much for this miracle machine. Seven hundred pounds, came the reply. Seven hundred? I can't afford that, my current cleaner cost me less than a hundred! That's why your house isn't clean… we have a very competitive finance package if you can't pay right away. I thought you were decent people, but perhaps you're typical Decken after all, how disappointing. No, I will not leave your filthy home until you have signed in this box, this one, this one, and this one, thank you so much. And if it wasn't the timesharers or Kayway it was double glazing firms and their indefatigable reps who never peed, slept or stopped talking, the sell-sell-sellers who swept away doubts with practiced blandishments, laid trails of false promises to lead the lost children into the witch's trap, the wolf's jaws. The fooled and their money were easily parted.

I couldn't stay; there was work to be done, but no paid work to be had. McLennan left the Project after a blazing row with its faceless management committee; I wondered if they feared for their windows. With stomach-knotting guilt, I applied for his vacant post, but this time I didn't survive the interview. The South it had to be, it seemed.

But I had grown fond of poor, exploited Decken, where I learned so many lessons. Not least:

Always appeal that decision.

Never let the rep into your home.

Never sign in that box.

Always keep the receipt.

Never accept the bloody credit note.

Purchasing Power

(i) The Joy of Spending (Midas)

It was a time of possibilities.

In 1987, the dole was about thirty pounds a week, the average weekly wage five times that. Thirty quid for a single man wasn't much, especially after three years of job-hunting in a town scoured clean of work by monetarist purism. The lucky, like me, threw themselves on helpful parents for handouts and somewhere to live; the unlucky scraped the bottom, unable even to settle, moved from B&B to B&B by callous, pointless rules. I offered myself silly, comforting, self-fulfilling thoughts—ahhh, it's just as well you can't get a girlfriend, after all, where could you go, what could you pay for? Better to wait, eh?

I was fed up with the trudge to sign on, the mind-battle in the Post Office, the blank walls in the Jobcentre where the vacancy cards were supposed to be. I spent a lot of time reading—too much, everyone thought—and after the government scheme at Decken Advice Project ended, I volunteered there. I trained as a debt adviser, but with the shades my old Maths teachers lining up to laugh the very idea to scorn. I swore I would never take on any such work. I revelled in benefits work, at last I felt as if I was of use to someone as I fought their corner, took on their appeals, and, more often than not, won.

There was a system, it was hostile, but beatable. My confidence soared, but then collapsed as time dragged but still no paid work appeared—*you can do this for other people, but what can you do for yourself? Nothing.* A cold sliver of Dragon ice had lodged in my flesh, and from time to time it twisted, an icicle goring.

After Decken, I had an apparent stroke of luck, paid work at another project, but this turned out to be a horrible mistake. I found myself working with people who made the Dragon look lovable; they scorned their clients, patronised and bullied their staff, paid and voluntary. I was back home on the dole again in a month, confidence and belief in myself near dead. Potential employers turned me down, half-promising to bear me in mind if a similar post came up. They were all lying—apart from Waveway Council.

I was not called to interview for a benefits advice job, but invited to see them about another offer—Consumer and Debt advice. I never panicked so much as when I took the call offering me the job; four years' search, it was all over, assuming I wasn't heading to another dragon-nest.

From thirty pounds a week to five times that; it was dizzying. The work was demanding, and I earned my money. More important for this treatise is that I learned how to spend it. I had been sidelined, powerless, for nearly five years: suddenly I was an economic actor, a customer, not just an adviser of consumers but someone who could *buy*, could *pay*. The bank was slap next door to my office, cash machine a stride away. I could slip in my card, flick my fingers and walk away with money, *my* money, pulled from a wall. And instead of having to queue to sign on, queue to cash the giro, slink away, my salary went straight into my bank, I didn't have to ask anyone.

I had a job, a serious one (and I was soon to find out just how serious), but there was serious spending to be done. A changed life. The Promissory had paid off at last. What next? No limits.

I could move to a shared house, pay rent, dream of my own place, buy books, *new* books and not just yellowed, torn fourth-hand ragged paperbacks, travel, get a round in—it may seem a small thing, but the ability to say 'I'll get these' without quailing was a landmark. I could pay for meals, get a taxi if I didn't want to walk or bus it, donate more than shamed coppers to charity, hold my head high. Perhaps I could get driving lessons—but even in my enhanced economic state, I quailed at the cost of running a car. I could buy clothes; with the exception of band and gig t-shirts I didn't, but it was a *possibility*, wasn't that what mattered?

It was the first time I'd saved since the long-ago days of the Saturday Sixpence. It was like being set free, given permission to exist. The feeling of liberation defeated the what-have-I-done quiver as I moved two hundred miles from home. I was served with the odd reminder that I was still an outsider of sorts—not fully-formed, economically. I applied to rent a washing machine, having embarrassed myself by admitting to someone I still took my laundry home when I visited at weekends, too self-conscious to go to a launderette, only to be refused the rental. And why? Because throughout my adult life to date I had left no footprint, I had no credit record; for them I didn't count, and you don't give credit to an invisible man.

I felt the lingering sting of that slap for longer than I should have, but it was only a minor setback on the road to full economic agency. I had… arrived. The feeling of personal importance going round the supermarket, my trolley stacked with goods, for which I would pay! *I exist! I spend therefore I am!* A character in a novel claimed that an Englishman's proudest boast was, 'I paid my way.' I could buy into that. Strut, pride, confidence. Purchasing power is a superpower.

A mini-Midas, that was me. But a moderate Midas too, not too much, not too little, no braggadocio, no cash-flashing; controlled gold. Perhaps the effect would wear off as I realised I was only a comparative Midas, an average-wager who had come up from nothing and was still dizzy with the rapid, heady elevation. Generous but not patronising, a force for good.

A colleague told me quietly there was too much month left at the end of their money and they didn't know what to do; just as quietly I offered to help, pay me back when you can. I'd never been able to do that before; friends had done it for me through those four long years, small things like going for a curry and not leaving me out just because I couldn't pay, paying for that round when I couldn't say 'I'll get these.' It felt good being the one able to help, but our secret chilled the working relationship for a time.

I was not so much a kid in a sweetshop as a record shop. No more vinyl hand me downs or asking a mate to tape something; no more studenty haunting of second-hand shops or saving to buy only the best of known favourites because I couldn't afford to experiment. If I wanted to try something different, I'd give it a go; if I wanted something new, I'd get it on its release date. I retired my worn-out portable record player and invested not just in a new deck, tape player, amp and speakers, but at last joined the modern audio world and acquired a CD player and my first shiny-new discs.

GoodPrice Records was my chief haunt; the shop was a prefab box in the Broad Walk, shopsigned by a large red plastic LP above its door, its glassy frontage filled with strung-up album covers, streamers made of silvery, sun-catching CDs. The newest, latest, waited patiently for me on the racks within, now within my grasp. I filled the little red metal shelves in my bedroom, and soon looked for somewhere to house the overspill. Narrow in my tastes during giro days, I became The Eclectic Man, who listened to and liked all sorts of music, freed from four-year money-shackles, from the conservatism of can't-afford.

It took a time for Purchasing Power to encounter its inevitable limits.

(ii) White Arrow (Can't Buy Me)

'Hey now, White Arrow. How goes the hunting?'

The crackle on the line could have been interference, or Matty's cough of a laugh.

'Same as ever.'

'Still never a shot fired?'

'Weeeeellll—nope.'

White Arrow.

It sounded like a real hunter's name, but it was only half of the nickname: the rest was Blue Background. Consult your Highway Code. Matty had labelled me WABB to mock the distinctly one-way nature of any notion of romance in my life. I had owned up about Michelle Ockendon; he knew about Durber. He gave me better advice than Big Jace would have (but then so could anyone), yet I still did nothing. I let her slip away to a new life in France, free from Monkey but never aware what was going on in my head.

'Anyone new to be admired afar?' Matty joshed. 'Missing Annettainable?'

'There is the smug sound of a lucky bastard who's got the perfect relationship.'

'Go on, you can tell me. Surely now you're a plutocrat they're queueing up?'

'No mate. And I won't do a Clifton either.' Matty choke-coughed again; Clifton used to follow women around his local nightclub waving his arms and yelling in a voice betraying weary desperation, 'I've *got money!*' Even Jace wouldn't have encouraged such behaviour. It didn't work.

'But you've got your eye on someone. I can just *tell*. Poor, sad White Arrow and his ever-frustrated quest.'

I furnaced a hot English A-Level sigh—and told him about GoodPrice records.

So, now: life was filled with work and soothed with music. But what was missing? What can't money buy? Come on, music fans. I was at GoodPrice again, buying three, or was it four, new albums, but my thoughts were elsewhere and I didn't look up as the figure behind the counter took the empty sleeves from me and went to the racks at the back of the shop to fill them. I couldn't do that job, I mused, I'd look in the wrong place, get the wrong inner sleeves, fumble, drop the discs, scratch them, clumsy-clumsy-me. There was a rapid bip-bip-bip as the good price was totted, but still I had my eyes and thoughts elsewhere.

'Oh sorry,' said a suitably musical voice, 'I forgot to take off the ten percent discount.'

'Discount?' I was dislodged from my distracting thoughts.

'DJ's discount... you're a DJ aren't you?'

I laughed, trying to kill off the cheapskate part of me that wanted to lie. 'Ah no, I work just down the corner there, I just like my music...' Having talked my way out of my ten percent, I readied to return to work.

'Your receipt's in the bag.' What a nice smile. What an appealing face. What a cool hand as she placed my change into my palm. Oh my goodness I'm looking at her, and going red. I remembered some of Big Jace's girl-hunting advice delivered across a pub table; 'Look em straight in the eye, ask open questions, don't let em yes or no ya, keep em talking, don't be too bloody eager, make em come after you…' Jace was also of the treat em mean keep em keen school. Thankfully I ignored his advice, but I also ignored my own better instincts, taking my records with a mumble-stumble thank-you and trying not to trip over myself as I left the shop.

Should I have said I was a DJ? But it would have been a lie, d'you want to start off with a lie? Jace and the other lads at home would advise lie-lie-lie, if it would get you anywhere. And while we're about it, your old 'thank goodness I haven't got a girlfriend' sophistry won't work anymore, there are plenty of places to go round here, all you needed was to ask. What use is Purchasing Power if it's not for this, eh? Why not say you forgot something, regain that eye contact, ask a cheeky-shy question? I rushed back to work, to tangle with problems at least nominally soluble.

Can't buy me courage.

Another opportunity: there was a new album by The Cocteau Twins (sweetdreamy indiemusic), another by Extreme Noise Terror (very much what it said on the tin); I handed over the empty sleeves to… it was her!

'Is one of these for someone else?' She smiled, playing up her incredulity.

'Ah, er… no.' Mumblestumble struck again.

'You can't *possibly* want them both!' That smile, that laugh, she was so lovely. *Go on*, advised Big Jace, you've started the conversation, you've got her interested, even better you've got her laughing; keep it going, eye contact, eye contact! You've done offer-acceptance-consideration buying the bloody records, now make a contract with her! And make sure you touch her hand when you take your receipt! Keep looking in her eyes!

Beautiful eyes. Limpid.

I pictured us at a restaurant, chatting, laughing. I'll get the bill; Purchasing Power is gallant, you see. I wanted a holiday but didn't want to travel alone; what if, what if, what if… I overdosed on possibilities, they carried me away, I lost the moment. I found my mouth had dried up and my tongue stuck fast. I managed some stupid comment about how I'd come back and tell her which record I liked better.

Did I ever find a storehouse of courage, go back and ask her out? Of course not; White Arrow, Blue Background. GoodPrice Records didn't help matters; it closed soon after and I never saw her again. I couldn't have spent enough there.

Can't buy me another chance.

(iii) Economy

'You know what you are? You're an *idiot* who makes *shit* decisions!' Matty's voice, usually all-over warm with the cadences of South-West England, was raised to a nails-on-slate screech as he lost his rag. In Eloise's place I would have burst into tears, but she was not for crying; her eyes welled, but it was with a cold, shocked, hurt, one of the sufferers of extreme injustice who would have her moment later. She had bought some throws for their worn-out furniture, to make their home prettier, what was wrong with that? Matty picked up on her unspoken rebuke, which only succeeded in making him angrier.

'Yeah, yeah, the suite's knackered and you think you're saving money, putting off buying a new one, but you *never* save money, you're *useless* with money. I have to go round the house closing doors to keep the heat in, switching off the Eloise Trail of Lights that shows your progress from room to room, turning the heating off constant, taking things off standby that you're allowing to trickle our money away, and as for the time you spend on the fucking phone… Even now you just look at me like that, you don't understand; *why* don't you understand?' His voice was filled with cruel, cold passion. I had never heard the like from him.

Eloise later confided that he demanded she ask permission before putting the water on for a bath, that he would check the cooker 'to make sure you've turned it off properly', patrolled the house to ensure windows were shut, changed their regular shop from aspirational DuRose to two-for-one Sayvit, checking the strips of till-roll with forensic care before paying and then hunching over them under a strong lamp once he got home, making frequent little inarticulate 'blame noises' as Eloise called them. They were on a water meter, so he would tighten dripping taps so hard she could not turn them back on, and he scowled if he saw her reach towards her bath towel. Above all, he insisted that dealings with their bank, their mortgage, be conducted strictly by him; as a gesture of trust, she consented, unhappily.

'Economy drive.' Eloise spread her hands helplessly. 'Obsessive. He's going up the ladder, getting paid more and more, but the better off he is, the bloody *tighter* he gets!'

Beers with Matty often became brotherly confessional sessions; I would tell him that Purchasing Power was all well, but loneliness was shadowing my new life and my self-mocking White Arrow tales of romantic ineptitude weren't making me laugh any longer. One evening, Matty touched on something new, from deep within.

'There's this… this *thing*, like a rising pain, growing all the time, it sits under my lungs, on top of my guts, it's trapped, but trying, constantly trying, to break out.'

'Wind?' My joke bombed.

'More like a scream, a trapped scream. If I could just let it out, where and when it wouldn't do any harm to anyone, but at the moment I'm hemmed in, surrounded by people, things. I'm afraid I'm going to blow up at the worst time, at someone I shouldn't.'

'You sure you're not already?' This played worse than the joke.

'I'm depressed,' he grunted, as if this explained and forgave all. 'I want to tell her… that it's not her.'

'So do it. Quick.'

'Can't. I just want to scream…'

'Okay, you've told me it's not her. So what is it?'

It was a time of impossibilities. The economy was in

trouble, but that wasn't so much an impossibility as the norm. The road to national recovery, the nostrum of the age, was that our country would become a property-owning democracy, each of us with our stake in the common good through the sterling ownership of four walls and a respectable, storm-proof roof. We would all be householders. Bricks and mortar not only embodied self-sufficient pride, but were also an eternal asset, never depreciating; house prices would rise and go on rising, and we would all gain from this graceful, benevolent, economic curve.

The graphic ending of this hyperbole came in the form of the Warrant Storm, in which proud owners could no longer pay their mortgages and faced homelessness. To cope with unexpected kinks in the great economic curve, the government increased interest rates to unexpected heights, which began a decline in house prices, and, concomitantly, the impossible; the value of people's houses fell below their outstanding mortgage debt when many of them found their monthly payments rising beyond their ability to pay. Arrears ticked up, lenders became concerned, then worried, then rather less friendly and understanding than their advertising would have you believe, then nakedly self-preserving as they repossessed properties on an unprecedented scale. The property-owning democracy was frantically heading to the doors of the repossession court.

All those stunned people: *How did it happen… to me?*

The other impossibility was that Eloise and Matty should part.

'What am I?' Matty glowered over another beer.

'Come on mate...' I protested.

'I'm an idiot who makes shit decisions.' His face was hangdog, funereal.

I sighed. It was like being at work, seeing people come in with their ballooning debts; the worry, shame, the need to blame, the hovering vulture-winged fear. Matty and Eloise really were struggling. If I was mini-Midas, they were the eternal golden couple, together ten years and everything had appeared ideal, their future path clear—marriage, a family, but, first, a foot on the property ladder. It was their misfortune that suddenly this rung was a dangerous place to be. When they signed their mortgage, interest rates were 8%: straight afterwards the rate climbed, then clambered, and was now touching 15%. The payments were crushing them.

Matty was an upward-curve kind of guy; give him good times and his smile arced; but give him bad and he was down in the mouth, an inverted horseshoe. Eloise was always glass half-full and waiting to be topped up, a quality Matty had previously found attractive; now her optimism irked him, that and a lot of other things, and he'd started to show it all too plainly. He became withdrawn, bitter, woundingly sarcastic in response to the most innocent queries. They were going to lose their home and it was *her* fault, *her* and her stupid middle-class aspirations. Eloise, stunned, defended herself half-heartedly and wondered dazedly what to do. On one of my visits to their flat I found a note, her-to-him, reminding him of happiness and love and good times, and how loving and trusting one another would always get then through hard times. He had thrown it into a corner.

Matty hinted heavily over a beer that the better things in their life had come courtesy of overtime, which was drying up like a puddle in the sun. His employers offered him a promotion and he was fool enough to take it; a 'manager' now, but guess what 'managers' didn't get? Any more pay, for one. And the other thing? No paid overtime—but of course the company wanted the extra hours from him anyway: that's what managers did.

'Always check the small print,' Matty horseshoed disconsolately, 'Unless, of course, you happen to be an idiot who makes shit decisions.' He glared at his beer as if lining it up for a share of culpability. 'We can afford to live—but not much more.' Visiting them had become an on-pins occupation, as he spoke unceasingly about strict economies, berating Eloise for her wasteful ways in front of me, in front of anyone; the relationship tipped towards disaster. The atmosphere grew worse as the interest rate racked up and the roof over their heads became less and less affordable.

'A bloody idiot.' Matty trudged back over the ground. 'She knows about the mortgage going up of course, but I told her it was okay—my promotion would cover it. Then I didn't tell her about the first arrears letter. Or the second. At least that way one of us could sleep.'

'Time to tell all?' I prompted.

'And say sorry, you mean?' His tone was brittle; I was being warned off.

'She'll understand. Which is more than she does now. All she knows at the moment is that she can't do right for doing wrong.'

'She'll leave me soon,' Matty moaned. 'Save me the effort of humiliating myself.'

'Tell her. G'won. You need to.'

Matty signalled stop-now, and glowered in silence for a while. 'You seeing this a lot?'

'Yes.'

'What's the routine? What's next? They come and foreclose on us or something?'

'No, that's more a USA thing. But they can send you a court summons, you fill in a response, explain your situation, and turn up on the date given.'

'I couldn't…'

'Best you do. Look, I'm always telling people, it's not hanging-judge time, it's a bloke or woman in a suit, no wigs, no big bench, no public gallery; it's a District Judge, they're most of them pretty feet-on-the-ground, they don't wanna kick someone out of their home, they'll look for ways to help. First thing they say to me and the solicitor on the other side at any hearing is, "Any chance of an agreement here?"'

'What sort of agreement?'

'Usually pay your current mortgage plus as much as you can off the arrears. If you can stick to that, they might award possession to the mortgage people, but it's suspended, long as you stick to the terms.'

'And if you can't?'

'You get about twenty-eight days then the lender can apply for a warrant. Eviction. But even that can be suspended if you can come up with a new offer.'

'It sounds too easy.'

'It isn't, but it can be done.'

'We're in negative equity. That won't help.'

'It doesn't. They can say their security is at risk, push for sale. But you can argue that values will go back up and they're being hasty.'

Matty sighed, saddened, regretful beer-breath across the table. 'I get so wound up, especially with not telling her. Keep imagining the scene when I do. Won't be me yelling then. It's just… I feel as if I could just shout, scream, loud enough, let it out, then something would change, I'd see clear of it, it would be okay…'

I let that go. No comment. Matty fell silent again, tussling another idea.

'Can't I just walk away?' Not 'we', I noticed, 'Can't I just hand in the keys and make an end of it?'

'Don't do it. You give them vacant possession but the debt's still there, the mortgage still runs, then they sell it for far less than you would get, and the bill follows you wherever you've run to. I've got a case on now, someone who walked, got landed with a demand for £45,000.'

'What if I just go bankrupt? That seems the fashionable thing at the minute.'

'Won't work if you're a homeowner; it's a shortcut to losing everything. My £45,000 debtor is thinking of bankruptcy—but that's now they've lost the lot and can't afford to pay.'

'I reckon I should just...' Matty gestured gun-at-head.

'Then you really *do* give them vacant possession.'

'So: we can't pay, we can't sell, we can't run. We're fucking screwed.'

'You and thousands more.'

'I don't care about *them*.' Petulant snap; the tone he used to Eloise.

'Tell her. You need to.'

'She'll leave me. She'd be better off leaving me. She should go off with some moneybags—you, you're one now.'

'C'mon mate, tell her. She loves you. Tell her about the strain, tell her why you've been like this...'

'She'll just go back to her cosy fantasies, everything'll be alright, she keeps leaving me notes saying love brought us together and life will see us through... her head lives in a fucking Disney film.'

'She's better than that, ask for her hel—'

Matty's eyes flashed, inner angry fire. 'If you want her, you can have her. You can afford her now.'

'That's not what—'

'But think what might happen if your little one-way shaft was returned? You wouldn't know what to do. Unlikely scenario, but funny to think of. Purchasing Power, eh? Good hunting, White Arrow.'

Matty would say nothing more. The brotherly, confessional moment was over. We both simmered.

(iv) The Goods On Display (Icarus)

Holiday weekends usually mean a steel-capped sky and rain in regular chilling pulses, but this time we were going to get away with it; the bright sky and hot sun, clear air, green fields, breeze, cried carefree. Optimistic signs for the beginning of my project. We exchanged our tickets for bright-green plastic wristbands; bound in place and feeling unbreakable, they were a real receipt, a memento, keepsake of good times returned. Purchasing Power was in a new phase. As Matty and Eloise were trapped within the four walls they had worked so hard to gain, I reasoned, what better than to get them outdooring? I had taken them out for a few meals, explaining I was paying back my mates who bought me curry when I was broke; they accepted with English humility and quiet, embarrassed resentment and so that plan perished. I needed a better, more focused intervention, I believed Purchasing Power could take the couple out of their troubles, revive our friendship and somehow ease, even heal, the breach between them.

The Bossage Festival was, once-upon, the place to be, where all the coolest bands played and happy, transported audiences frolicked without regard to the scorching sun, rods of rain, or the fields of mud; but as light years turned into leaden decades, it became little more than a pickling jar for fading careers, a turgid day out geared more to desperate, clinging reminiscence than the enjoyment of the new and the now. After a financial crisis—who hadn't had one?—Bossage was bought out by new people with fresh ideas, the festival revived, the past laid to rest, the present and to-be given centre stage.

It helped that on both days, big favourites of Matty's were lined up. I was happy as we made our way into the showground, Matty and Eloise walking together and me wandering ahead, daydreaming harmlessly of the girl from GoodPrice records strolling by my side. I wore the best and brightest gig t-shirt from my collection and ludicrous baggy shorts Eric Morecambe would have envied: my image said 'this person is here for a good time, he isn't serious about *anything*'. Except, keenness to witness the healing work of Purchasing Power.

The festival ground between the gates and the distant, heat-haze-wavering mirage-esque stage, was like a small market town, bordered with burger and ice cream vans, beer tents, food stalls: almost as much as on the stage, the showground centred on row upon row of pop-up stalls. Clothing, gig t-shirts, bags, hats, bootleg tapes and discs, jewellery, hair decorations, bangles, bands, beads, candy floss, fringed jackets, shoes, boots, clogs, wellies for the rainy days, glow sticks, balloons, concessions of all sorts. Families threaded between the stalls, small children on parents' shoulders, couples dallied hand in hand, arm in arm, shoulder-nudging, pointing, laughing, kissing, wandering on. The air smelt of mown grass, fried onions, leather, spices, flavoured steam, sugar, puffs of dope. The breeze blew music towards us as the first bands set up and kicked off. Still the stage seemed unreal, unreachable.

Eloise wore sandals, a long skirt and a t-shirt, a tie-dye fractal swirl of infinity-teddies; her hair was braided, her neck adorned with a thin, fluttering yellow-red scarf. Matty walked close by her, but he shook off her proffered hand and dodged affectionate gestures increasingly sulkily, like a schoolboy fending off his mum because his mates are watching. He was unshaven, dressed head to foot in black, his face again lugubrious, his mouth a bad-luck horseshoe. He joked that he looked like a villain from a Western who'd lost his hat and horse, it was a laughless jest. He described Eloise as showing her true self, a beautiful hippie chick who belonged in the lost past, which sounded flatly insulting. She didn't react; inured to it perhaps, hanging on and hoping, or past caring.

'She knows about the decisions.' Matty muttered to me as Eloise lingered over a stall selling leather-thong amulets, 'And their shitness.'

'Has that cleared the air?'

'She talked a lot about love. Not entirely sure what it meant. Love won't keep the bailiffs out. We shouldn't be here; we should be pushing wardrobes up against the front door.'

'I know what you're doing.' Matty pronounced, ending a protracted silence.

'Trying to steal your girlfriend, according to you.'

'Nahhh, that's not it. Maybe you wouldn't mind if she fell to you naturally like a little plum off a tree, but

I don't think that's your game, really. Big day out, sunshine, music, just like old times, and as night falls, she and I will rekindle happily by the light of a Tiki Torch. That's what you've bought, moneyman. Correction, what you *think* you've bought.'

Another Pinterian pause.

'Who made you the matchmaker—White Arrow?' Matty hummed a few bars of *Stupid Cupid* and looked pleased. 'If your plan works, I can't say she'll thank you in the long run. Me neither.'

'That's up to you.'

'Quick lesson in economics, mate.' Matty added, sighing heavily.

'Economics?' interrupted Eloise brightly, as she wandered to a nearby stall. 'He knows *nothing* about it! Beware of bad teacher!' She laughed lightly.

Matty scowled. I waited for his wisdom. 'Like I say, I know what you're trying to do. You're trying to spend your way out of trouble. Lots of companies, governments even, have tried it. Usually doesn't end well; often as not you just buy yourself more and worse.' I thanked him for the lesson, without any edge to my voice.

Eloise was dangling long earrings, pinched in her fingers. They caught the sunlight and sparkled steel, emerald, sapphire. 'Plastic and old tin cans,' Matty opined in my ear. He walked to Eloise and she drooped one of the earrings by her lobe, posing, ready to laugh. Matty walked past her and inspected the prices, set out in little sticky tickets on the velvety display stand.

'Half a week's food shopping,' Matty told her flatly,

stalking away to watch the crowd filtering by, edging towards the stage but diverted into rivulets from time to time, talking, chatting, laughing, regaining their flow, slowly onwards. Matty was fascinated by the people, especially the women. 'It's good here,' he admitted grudgingly. 'It's always interesting to see the goods on display.' As he had his back to the stall and his eyes on bare shoulders, legs, midriff, semi-transparent skirts, elegant necks, faces filled with youthful vigour and beauty, there was no doubt what was on his mind. Little doubt, too, that Eloise had heard him, that he had intended his voice to carry. 'Tell you what, White Arrow.' Matty pointed and leered at a passer-by who was backlit by the strong, friendly sun. 'Heard of VPL? Well *there* is a case of V*P*. And very nice too.' This time there was no doubting it: Eloise had heard. She turned away, refusing to be provoked. I hoped.

Acheron ground out semi-distant doom tunes. I liked Acheron and wished I was up by the stage, but a nauseated fascination held me in place, witnessing what I had bought. Still flesh-watching, Matty extended an all-encompassing arm. 'These are no good to you, you can't appreciate them. You'd need to pick one, weave her into a story, make her unobtainable, fail to climb the tower to rescue her, break your heart over her, sobbing on the ground. *I* could walk over to any one of them— *any one of them*—and I'd be away with her. Brief and to the point, no romantic build-up, no goo-goo eyes, no millsyboonsy narrative needed.' We approached a little nearer to the music.

Eloise drifted to another stall and tried on a rainbow

poncho, giving a windmill twirl, laughing; the poncho allied with the t-shirt made her look as if she had been coloured in by a child. She was beautiful.

'You're making a fool of yourself.' Matty muttered to her, and her playful smile was snuffed. She pulled at the poncho and returned it roughly to the trader, as if it were he who had given offence. Matty's attention had wandered; he was giving a hard stare to an over-exuberant group of lads elbowing their way past the idling shoppers, yelling *'Mosh Pit!'* My old friend reminded me of my beloved grey-muzzled terrier when she reached fourteen or fifteen; baring fangs, growling with dangerous disapproval at young puppies whose only sin was to want to play in the sunshine.

The next act was on, someone had turned up the volume and at last I could hear more than smothering bass at one end and tin-can cymbals at the other. Matty didn't seem drawn by the music, and I was held back by my thoughts, my fears. Eloise had at first appeared to be trying to make the best of things but in my view, she was now going out of her way to annoy Matty. Admittedly that didn't take much, but she was choosing her ground, working out what he'd hate most. She inspected more leather-thong jewellery, shooting me an amused look when Matty spluttered at the price-tags. She bought candy floss for herself and me, revelling in his disapprobation at such infantile fairground behaviour; she offered to run her sticky fingers through his hair and he ducked, a sour teenager dodging his maiden aunt. Eloise found this hilarious and chased him until he begged her to stop. It was the ritual of a courtship going backwards, unravelling.

We passed a tent with a pantomime mystic-east look about it, a board offering the delights of various forms of relaxation. 'I always fancied a reiki massage.' Eloise held out a hand towards the tent, as if testing its emanations, 'Get my chakras unblocked.'

Matty choked inarticulately. His rejoinder that perhaps he could get a naked massage from some 'oiled-up bird' sounded puny, whiny. When Eloise found a fortune teller, she didn't even say anything, didn't gesture, just grinned. Matty's mouth varied between a hard, flat line and the unlucky horseshoe. He still muttered occasionally, but between his teeth, to himself. Stall by stall, item by item—crap, junk, expensive shite, unnecessary, extravagant, frivolous—Eloise dallied and Matty complained. They were all cheats, frauds, rob-dogs, and he was their victim; she, their shill.

Kickfever bounced onstage, yelled 'Hello Bossssage!' and made the ground shake; Matty glared at his erstwhile favourites as if they were in his garden uninvited. We were at the edge of the crowd, at last with the music, but even that failed. Eloise danced, draining Matty of even more joy, stoking his scowls. How did the mob around us manage it? Leaping, surging, dancing, pogoing, passing stage-divers overhead, dropping them to their feet, when the ground was so obviously sown with landmines? I was afraid to step forward-back-left-right; an explosion was imminent. Instead of a big bang, I saw a wave coming. In unison, people dipped their heads forward and then threw themselves backwards-up, some doing star-jumps, the tide swept through the crowd; Eloise leapt, I surged, the wave rushed on, but one object remained immovable; the motion had swept around Matty and he had resisted with a scowl at each and every fool; he glared at me and Eloise, silently berating our wanton foolishness. I had thought—silly magical-money thinking—that the closer we got to the stage, the closer I would get to success, but Matty was chilling even the music, he was resistant, impervious. His only joy was ogling the bouncing backsides of shoulder-hoisted girlfriends, the joggling breasts of dancers, swaying hips, legs—bare, stockinged, swish-skirted.

'The goods on display!' Matty's voice hoisted above the band. 'Good work, White Arrow, you didn't mean it—but you've shown me what to do.'

The music fell away.

'I,' pronounced Matty, 'am on the market.'

Between acts, we decided to look for something to eat, wandering back towards the burger-donner-pizza vans on the edges of the showground. It was leadenly predictable by then, but nothing pleased Matty; falafels with chilli sauce—no; curry in a cone—don't be silly; calzone—too expensive; chips—don't fancy them, greasy crap; salad wraps—I'm not a fucking rabbit and I'm not paying that much either.

'There are plenty of other places we can try,' Eloise tried a bright tone.

Grit-toothed, angry as if she had been the one who

had cavilled and objected to everything, Matty cut across her, hissing; *'Find* something!'

'You have got a lot of sorrys to say for this weekend,' Eloise scolded in a bitter whisper.

Matty put his face close, as if to kiss, and sneered. 'There's only one thing I'm sorry about. And that's fixable.' Now I understood his economics—the world had cheated Matty, someone had to pay. If he didn't before, he understood the transactional nature of life; someone has hurt me, I am powerless to get back at *them*—so you will do.

I Understand That Machine played the best set I had ever heard from them; Matty gave no impression of listening, no recognition of songs he had loved for years. After three encores, the band left an unattended guitar howling in loops of clamouring air-clawing sound, abandoning their equipment and slinking off as if they knew how deeply they'd disappointed Matty. Fire-bouquets rocketed up from behind the stage, blossoming, blooming high above the cheering crowd. We three strolled from the festival ground, Matty ambling ahead of me and Eloise, making a pantomime show of ogling the slow-moving boobs and bums of the half-light.

Eloise drew me aside. 'You probably don't want another lesson in economics, but here it comes: the law of diminishing returns.'

'Dimi—'

'The harder I've tried, the less I've got from him. There comes a point at which there is… no *point*.'

'Dimi—'

'He's made a mistake—oh I know he has, not just the job, I know about the mortgage—but rather than come clean, he's decided it's all over whatever he does: so he's decided to tear everything down and see what rises from the wreckage—which is another economic concept, come to think of it. An ugly one, in my opinion. Anyway, diminishing returns, eh? Stop trying. I have.'

I could hear the guitar-loop, round and round, all the way out of the festival ground. I would not keep the wristband, the receipt. We would never come here again.

The Bottom of The Bag

(i)   Unlucky dip
(ii)   They bring it on themselves
(iii) Shouters and quiet menace
(iv) Bright t-shirts
(v)   Suits (the Warrant-Storm)
(vi) Mr and Mrs Saxon's day in court
(vii) Bankrupt at 2.15 pm
(viii) The Innocents

(i)

It was always the last appointment of the day. With part-hopeful, more-shamed looks, they would produce the big plastic bag into which they had scooped every fold and tatter of paper they could lay their hands on. Gathering papers to present them to the scrutiny of a stranger took a special courage; these were people who had learned to freeze like hunted animals at the rattle and clank of the letterbox, to take the terrible envelopes and put them away 'till later', to tremble as they opened them, should they ever dare, to scrabble after excuses not to do so, oppressed by a hopeless longing to light a fire and toss them in. To cram these things together, even if only to dump them in disarray into the biggest plastic shopper in the house. It was a hard, heartbreaking abnegation of pride, exposing secrets they had hoped somehow-somehow would never emerge. Walking naked down a crowded street would have been simple by comparison.

Take the bag, plunge in your hand, delve.

The thing that mattered most was always at the bottom of the bag.

Time and again, delve, and come up with tissues, tatters, letters used as shopping lists, appointments forthcoming and gone, assorted receipts, red block-capital threateners, gothic-script demand-tirades from chancers and line-shooters, cheque stubs, brief, coolly-worded epistles from those who could do the real damage, catalogue accounts, court judgments, credit card statements, the occasional scribbled love note or child's crayon drawing, recipes, the inevitable Provy book, and there, at the bottom: the warrant.

It was unimpressive; no red letters, no gothic script or florid language or threats, simply a statement of a date and time at which bailiffs would attend to evict the occupants and change the locks. Deadly danger in plain clothing. Sometimes that date and time, though close, was far enough away for us to do something; it was possible even at the last minute to apply to the court to suspend the warrant, hold off the eviction, make an offer of repayment. Sometimes, though, the bailiffs were setting out to their work even as the householders were over-tightly clutching that large shopping bag in our waiting room.

Most were paying their debts, or trying to, even if it was a promise-excuse here and a payment there, a switch to next month, attempting not to annoy everyone, pay up/default on a panicky, improvised cycle. But always-always they were paying the wrong ones, those who shouted loudest, threatened most, used red ink and gothic script, or banged on the door, rousing the neighbourhood with ringing accusations. The red-letter shouters and extravagant threateners were the reason the people came for advice, to see the adviser in the bright t-shirts, the one with the pop-band posters on his office walls, who argued that the last thing people wanted to see was some posh besuited character who'd make them feel small. Nobody knew who to pay. It came as a shock to many when they found out who really could take their home, their goods, their liberty. The terse letters, with no wasted words, were the ones to fear; the plain-clothes, plain-words warrant being one of the deadliest. The rest were hyenas, howling but toothless.

Plunge in your hand, delve. There's a treat at the bottom of the bag.

Oh, sorry.

I left out a 'h'.

A reverse lucky-dip.

There but for the grace of… no, wait… how about… that could be me (or you), any time.

Ah yes, that will do.

(ii)

'Don't you *think* these people bring it on themselves?' The Ice Dragon posed her question with characteristic arctic emphasis and a fanged, stalagmite smile. She had already greeted me by using my surname, which was guaranteed to get my back up. Now she had heard what I did for a living, and pounced. That I was now employed was preferable to my previous state, but the nature of my work appalled her. Good.

'I've met one or two who admit they "just went mad" when given too much credit, but that is as much the fault of the credit companies. But I *think* most people I see have had a change, a drastic one, in their lives. Someone leaves, arrives, falls ill, dies. A job ends without warning. What was affordable yesterday is beyond reach today. That's why most of them are in trouble.' The temperature fell further. You didn't dispute with the Ice Dragon. 'A lot of people have got nothing in the first place; many others are so close to the precipice it doesn't take much to push them over. And when pushed, there's every chance they will never scramble back.'

Dragon's lip curled. 'I think your employers could spend their money better.' She sashayed away as if in triumph, having put my corner of the world to rights.

But nobody, *nobody* is safe. I cast a silent riposte after her, grenade-fashion—*not even you*. Someone leaves, falls ill, dies. That's all it takes, and over the edge we can all go. Even people who think they are secure, Dragon.

You won't believe how quickly prosperity can turn to vapour, gone no matter how desperately you claw, cry out, entreat. May you never know that plummet, Madam, and may we never have this conversation again; may we never speak again.

Judge not, eh, Dragon? Oh well; everyone needs a hobby.

(iii)

Siren voices everywhere.

Posters on hoardings, passing by on buses, on the radio, the TV, in shop windows.

WHY WAIT? TAKE IT NOW!
WHY BROWSE WHEN YOU CAN BUY?
INSTANT CREDIT AVAILABLE
0% FINANCE
BUY NOW—PAY LATER

A credit card company ran a TV slot in which Potless Pete dreamed of a holiday, a magical blue-water hot-sun getaway: empty pockets, what to do? Produce the plastic, urged Pete's pal, and, dissolve to a new scene, there they were on a white sand beach, paddling in toe-tickling paradisical waves.

The adverts never mentioned what might happen if you 'took it now' but were still potless when the bills arrived, or if in-between times someone leaves, dies, falls ill.

It was interesting to see how quickly, like the worst

of fair-weather friends, the moneymen descended, the very people who had fuelled and encouraged the spending; how their cheery tone transmuted, hardened into cold words and abrupt demands. Misleading letters would follow, and if people misperceived that a debt collector (no more rights than you or I to enter someone's home in pursuit of monies owed) was a bailiff (with some rights of entry but by no means the demigod powers imagined by most, including the bailiffs) then why should that debt collector discourage the mistake? If they waved a piece of paper (a letter from their mum, a takeaway menu, scrap plucked off a desk as they left the office) and dropped a hint that their next visit would be more 'official', if some of their operatives dressed a little like policemen, it was only a teensy-weensy deception, they weren't trying to scare anyone, they just wanted their clients' money, fair and square, y'know? It wasn't their problem if the debtor gulped in terror of arrest, dispossession, eviction, perhaps even a pelting in the stocks?

Everyone was distracted by the red-letter shouters, the threateners, the overcoloured, attention-seeking clownfish, while the real saw-toothed monsters lurked at the bottom of the bag: short but sharply-focused letters from the ones who could take your home (landlord or mortgagee) or cut off your supply (gas, electricity, water too, in those days) and, much to everyone's surprise, imprison you (everyone knew about court fines: the shocker was the Council Tax—Poll Tax most people still called it, still do—oh, and the Revenue, if they were feeling mean).

Some favoured frontal assault; lurid letters and door-banging, phonecalls-phonecalls-phonecalls. Others preferred to sit back and set traps, sending ambiguously worded short letters, 'MessageCable' one firm called itself, 'Wings of Gabriel' another: *Call This Number! We Have News!* Anyone sufficiently incautious, taking the chance that good luck was about to kiss them firmly on the lips, would find out that the news in question was *'Gotcha!'* The competition over the pickings, however thin they may have been, was intense. The shouters would try any tactic: threat, distraction, misinformation, disinformation; *we advise you not to seek advice, they will tell you lies, listen only to us.* Quite often they didn't have to try hard; just the tiniest push to trigger the debtors' already overactive imaginations. The people who had always known they were close to the abyss found the demands like buzzing flies, one more annoyance among life's many, but the people with vaporised dreams were puzzled and hurt, dazed by their fall and by the swipes and kicks they received as they tried to pick themselves up off the ground. They stuffed the big bag full of papers and came to the office, hoping that therein lurked a miracle-worker.

Anatomy of a misleading letter

Sent to a Mr Bowles of Waveway Town. Mr Bowles is purely fictional, but this style of letter is not. Mr Bowles is unemployed and living on benefits. He has no savings, no spare income after the basics of life are paid for. The debt collection firm is aware of this fact. They have refused his offer to pay £1 a week to show that he is willing but unable to pay.

Fairpay Collections
Justitia House
High Court
Stintonby
Wibbs

> Company name implies the debtor is being 'unfair' in being unable to pay.
>
> Intimidating intimations that 'Justice' has arrived at his door at last.
>
> Carefully chosen misleading address implying the company is part of the court system when it is not.

Dear Mr Bowels,

> Carefully mis-spelt name; a small, deniable insult. Just a slip; sorry.

NOTIFICATION OF ENFORCEMENT OF DEBT [*This line is in red, bold, of course.*]

You are indebted to Principal Personal Loans Ltd to the sum of **£405.00** which is payable **WITH IMMEDIATE EFFECT** *[Red, bold.]*

You are advised to contact us **AT ONCE** [red, bold] to remit. Failure to pay **WITHIN THE NEXT FORTY-EIGHT HOURS** *[Red, bold]* will mean one of the following actions will be taken against you:

[all below in red, bold]

- the issuing of a writ in the courts
- the removal of your goods to settle the debt
- we will file for your IMMEDIATE BANKRUPTCY
- a Garnishee Order to remove funds from your bank account
- an order for Attachment of Earnings
- an order for you to be examined in open court as to your finances

> None of the enforcement actions can be taken until and unless the debtor has broken a court order to pay, and never without the permission of the court.
>
> 'Removal of goods' cannot be done by Fairpay. They need to obtain a court warrant and pay its bailiffs to act. This action can be suspended on application, for the court to be shown why the debtor cannot pay.
>
> The debt is too small for the debtor to be made bankrupt. But what the hell?
>
> The company knows the debtor is unemployed and has no money, so there is no account to Garnishee, no earnings to Attach, and 'Oral Examination' is an equally empty threat – it is used only for people who may be hiding assets and refusing to pay.
>
> But it's all good, scary stuff, and 'Mr Bowels' is now ready to get blood from a stone, in the form of another high-cost loan, to avoid whatever imagined fresh hell Fairpay may unleash.

If we could shout down the shouters, call the bluff of the loudest, we could help the person regain some control in their lives; they didn't have to borrow to pay off previous borrowings and so on in an eternal spiral of monetary reductionism: they could budget essentials, creditors, the shouters among them. As my old mate McLennan once told Decken's version of FairPay Collections, 'Ye're gettin' an equitable distribution of available income. In your case that's about ten pee a month. Now whist ye.'

(iv)

The Reception desk was a near-circle that could seat four, five at busy times (though staffing constraints meant it was usually only two at a time). The walls were covered with pinned papers (health advice, where to get help, did-you-know posters). The door sighed open and dragged itself shut on an erratic someone-coming automation, and in winter it made the whole room cold. A window facing out onto the main street looked like the side of a fish tank and the light from it was somehow yellowed, as if made old by delay, as though we were peering out into the recent past. A window facing East was tall and lozenge-shaped, letting in a more cheerful, immediate light, looking out over the Market Square. At the right time, when everything was aligned, you could see the full moon loom over a nearby low-rise tower; the sight was melancholy in its beauty. People could come through that door with any sort of problem—from 'where is the nearest GP surgery'—'do you have a map of the town'—'where's the pub'—to 'can I talk to someone in private, it's really urgent, no I can't wait for an appointment.' We would answer any public questions over the desk, and in our upstairs offices see people about confidential matters: unfair dismissal, benefit appeals, debt; things that had become the intractable everydays of the early 1990s.

It was full of characters. Taciturn, indomitable Nige, who took on the toughest cases, fuelled by cigarettes and cool determination; his admiring clients said that he hailed from 'The Clint Eastwood School of advice work'. Siddiq, who on his turn on reception would try to involve reluctant colleagues in long conversations about philosophy, meanwhile observing the people moving like chess pieces across the square flagstones of the market; if he saw someone struggling to walk, he noted their difficulties, the pain they were in, the slowness of their gait, their problems with balance, and he shot out of the door, caught up with them and demanded to know if they had yet applied for Mobility Allowance. Jerry would sing all day, songs from the shows, the oldies, sentimental ballads, his voice cheerful but every note hammered flat, yet with his colleagues he affected a surly disdain, interrupting conversations to tell us how wrong we were (whatever the topic), and if we liked something—music, books, TV, cinema—rubbish it, always implying that there was not just something off-colour but a quality of cultural evil about what we favoured. Brynna, on Reception, would greet Jerry every day with a bright 'Good Morning!' and, on hearing his grunted, truculent reply, follow him around the building goodmorninging with determined repetitiousness until she received an acceptably polite response. Trevelyan, usually dressed as if gone fishing, would listen languidly as aggrieved workers cursed the bosses who had sacked them, cut their pay, treated them like dirt. 'They can't *do* that to me!' the enraged one would cry. 'Yeah but, they just *did*, didn't they?' Trevelyan doused their ardour, but usually won their cases.

One employer, Mr Ransomme, was in the habit of phoning Trevelyan once a month, saying 'You bastard' then slamming the phone down. When Ransomme died, Trevelyan missed him terribly. Characters, problem-solvers, eccentrics, fighters all; people who knew there was a battle out there worth winning, and only our ragtag army around to help even the score in an unfair world. How well the great McLennan would have fitted in there. We all knew: you can't save everyone, but you can make a difference.

I was the adviser who wore jeans, baseball boots and the band and gig shirts bought with Purchasing Power; my outfit was echo-flattery of Matty's style, also representing the fading of my attempts to be young and unconventional. I had already tried to appease the angry spirits of the age having my hair cut to a respectable length, although to my chagrin I had found out that I would have secured this job even with the tumbling locks. Yet I was already conceding more ground; yes, I'd ditch the t-shirts, yes the jeans and sneakers, maybe later, maybe later, when I'm thirty, not yet. Time would press me into sartorial sobriety, just as it would gradually wear away the youthful enthusiasm that earned me the nickname Tigger. It was my job to broach that deep bag, separate the mangle-tangle of papers, explain to worried people what constituted a priority debt.

The bright t-shirts were an almost-selling-point: as I argued, I was causal, approachable. The shirts spoke the times: a bright blue background, a flower, black letters J-a-m-e-s; the eye-dazzling shirt from U2's 'Achtung Baby' tour; My Bloody Valentine's 'Loveless'. I accepted, reluctantly, the advice that wearing my Wonder Stuff 'IDIOT' t-shirt may undermine clients' confidence. At one point there was a call from a well-known consumer advice show, asking for 'the adviser in the bright t-shirts'. I didn't get on TV.

Two fingers to the Dragon and the other nagging voices who said I would never work, never do anything of worth. This was me, being valuable to a community even if I couldn't be to my own, and this time someone had sufficient confidence in my abilities to pay me to do it. It didn't abolish the voices of doubt because they were inset, ingrained, part of me, but to feel valued, to be a professional and not just a volunteer, that gave uplift, assurance, confidence. And, to begin with, that Tiggerish bounce. I would sometimes jump and slide across that big desk, the better to fetch a leaflet or answer a phone, pull the door open for a visitor when the mechanism failed.

I was in the South, but even in that legendary job-orchard, things could go wrong; 'pockets of deprivation' was a fashionable phrase. We were in the third most deprived area in the South. For a time, our political masters shared our idealism and energy, an Anti-Poverty Strategy was put in place, a local-only measure, as we had an Ice Dragon government that blamed the poor for poverty and prescribed harsh measures to force self-reliance. Lone parents were the target of the day; cut their benefits, make them work, they only get pregnant for council housing, etcetera-etcetera, accusations on and on. That someone may have left, died, was not allowed into this narrative. It was wonderful for us as advisers to win individual triumphs, but we all knew something broader was needed, something better that broke downward spirals, changed the condescending views of the powerful: that would give people the power to oppose landlords who refused to repair damp, unhealthy homes, stopped parents having to eat beans on toast so their children may enjoy decent meals, allowed people to budget for clothing without seeking charity, made home insurance affordable so that the least fortunate didn't suffer the most from misfortune.

Low incomes meant an inability to pay for the best food, and the enduring grip of cheap, unhealthy rubbish. People who were ill needed medicines, but anyone not on the lowest benefits had to pay in full for prescriptions and the costs rose year by year; the TV Licence was compulsory, backed with fines, but without any rebate for the worst off. Worse, its enforcers would prosecute whoever opened the door of an unlicensed property, and if it was a visitor, friend, neighbour, they cared not. And in the murk, out there beyond the magic touch of any adviser, no matter how clever or persistent, were the sharks of the species Loan. Our regular opponents were at least licensed to practice their trade and ultimately within the reach of the law, but these creatures had no office address, didn't write letters, and collected debts without troubling the courts. Someone with more power than us had to land these monsters.

There were cases of long-lasting, intractable difficulty, there was nothing in the world bar wand-waves or a Lottery payout that would change the lives of some of the more ground-down. Mrs Demane came in regularly, she worked endless hours but always complained in a drained, hopeless voice, 'I've got *no* money...' Whenever she was paid, there was someone there with their hand stuck out, or something broke and needed replacing, the children needed new clothes, the rent was due, the rates, the taxes. She earned too much to qualify for benefits, but far too little to be anything but poor. I was frustrated by my inability to make any difference; our regular meetings were enervating for both of us, this was her past, present, future. She could, I'm sure the Dragon and her ilk would argue, have got another job, but she would very likely have ended up like Mr Bulrose, a man with three jobs, or four, but as there was no minimum wage he could have had a string of employers and still not made ends meet.

Ill-luck stalked some: irony stung others. Mr Pickmere was a regular, drowning in debt, his creditors were especially unrelenting, regarding negotiation as a sign of weakness; he saw no way out other than insolvency, that or a very serious bunk. The day he went bankrupt, he won the Lottery; £50,000. Mr Pickmere never saw a penny, the Official Receiver took it all, and

Mr P was back to being an ordinary, blameless, penniless but debt-free citizen. Had that win come just a little earlier, perhaps we really could have negotiated for him to keep… just a little. All of them were surrounded by doorstep lenders who would give them enough to tide them over, enough to bind them into yet another debt, and any improvement in their pay became an increased pay-out at the not-so-friendly knock on a Friday.

Sometimes it was funny, if confusing, to be young and enthusiastic in that time and place. One afternoon I came down to the desk to ask the next person to come up for their appointment, and a birdlike figure upped and bobbed straight towards me; a small woman of about sixty years of age, the lines on her face more those of worry than age; like many people I spoke to, she looked concerned, perturbed, assailed by worries that perhaps, just perhaps, I could resolve.

'How *old* are you?' Piercing dark birdseyes, sharp, interrogative movements of the head.

'Erm…twenty-five.'

'Hmph. I disapprove of the modern way of morality you know; the way people behave these days. It seems to me that you agree with it. I will not see your sort.' The door sagged open in disbelief as she hopped towards it. I never did know what help she needed.

Mrs Armon was forever receiving Notices Seeking Possession from her landlord, scraping together just enough to call the dogs off, she never quite kept up with her rent; try-this try-that solutions came to nothing, and I dreaded appointments with her, as they dragged on for an hour at a time, fruitless renegotiations between irreconcilable blocs. As McLennan once put it, it was 'like beating your head against a sponge'. On my last Friday before a week's holiday, I blocked out the last two hours of the afternoon to tidy up the paperwork a little. At four o'clock, Brynna called me to say Mrs Armon had arrived for her appointment, she had assured Mrs A I wouldn't mind this last-minute arrangement. I braced, composed my face, trudged downstairs to face my fate, to be faced with only Brynna and Siddiq, grinning triumphantly and wishing me a happy holiday.

One morning Mrs Armon telephoned, voice bright with renewed hope. 'I've had a win on the Lottery.'

Great news! A few hundred? A Thousand? Several? As big as Mr Pickmere's and with no one poised to snatch it away? Enough to buy a house? Enough to be free of her troubles and perhaps help others too?

'Ten pound!'

'Ten…' My voice took on a whirring, grinding, run-down-motor sound. I made polite noises, and put the phone down without telling her I was contemplating coming round to break all her windows.

Where there is idealism, energy and enthusiasm, there is always a countervailing force; it manifests as the it's-no-use lobby, the it's-only-a-sticking-plaster whybotherers, people who perennially called for us to be shut down, the acolytes of the Ice Dragon who thought it was all a waste of money; those who wished to jump ahead to the chapter 'In Which Tigger Is Unbounced'. We relied on the whimmish will of politicians, but the future became clear when one of their number, a self-styled 'workers' representative', called for us to 'stop celebrating deprivation'. We argued that we 'celebrated' deprivation as Muhammad Ali 'celebrated' his opponents, but the political weather was changing: poverty was to be shoved into the shadows; give it a hat, mask, dark glasses, fake whiskers, call it something else or, better, simply stop talking about it and it will go away.

(v)

Collar up; make sure you've done up the top button, no complaining, it won't choke you, it's your own fault for having a fat neck. Now: broad end over the right side, narrow end on the left; broad end longer than narrow but not by too much, how does it go, rabbit, tree, over there round there, tighten, straighten, that's one fat uneven rabbit you've got there. Try again and you've got a skinny lump in a long string. Or was the rabbit-tree thing another sort of knot? I hate this, always did. And I never could do my shoes up properly. Why the hell didn't I buy slip-ons, after all I'm Mr Purchasing Power, making my own decisions? I hadn't suffered this struggle since school, barring the odd wedding. Whoever invented ties has my undying enmity. What's the *point* of them? Well, because Judge Renfrew would be cross if you did not wear one, let that suffice. The bright t-shirts, jeans, baseball boots, all had to go back in the wardrobe; a suit was called for. You really don't want to go in front of Renfrew wearing a shirt saying IDIOT, do you? Well, no.

I liked Judge Renfrew; I was a little in awe of him, but I liked him and his fellow judges; as I had told Matty, they were judges but they were not the remote, desiccated creatures of famous old cases and TV fiction, clueless about life outside the dusty confines of lawbooks. They had power over people's lives but they didn't abuse it, they were realists, they tried to help the vulnerable, confused people who came before them. They stood for no nonsense; after listening to a perorating solicitor testing out his courtroom cadences, Judge Renfrew heaved a heavy, weary sigh and cut him off with, '*Do* stop trying to be Perry Mason…' He never commented on my appalling tie-knotting, but he had something to say about my handwriting. Glaring at a hastily scribbled application to save someone's home, Renfrew transferred the glare to me and threw the paper across the table.

'You wrote this—*you* read it!'

'I apologise, Sir. The more I use computers, the worse my handwriting gets.'

'Then I recommend you desist from using computers at once, young man.'

Judge Harlow was a far less grave figure, kindly and teacher-like, at least until she detected nonsense from either side of the table. I had spent some difficult minutes before a hearing trying to persuade a tenant on Income Support to offer to pay £2.50 a week off her rent arrears; it was more important to make an affordable offer that could be sustained than a large panic-offer on which payments would stutter and we would all end up back here before a much less forgiving judge; but the tenant was insistent.

'The offer is current rent—paid by Housing Benefit—plus five pounds a week.'

'Don't be foolish, this lady is on Income Support. Possession suspended on terms; current rent plus *two pounds and fifty pence* a week.' It was good to be able to tell tremulous defendants that the judges were human, that there was no big courtroom, no wigs or gowns, no being examined crossly, no jury, press or public, definitely *no* cameras—the proceedings would be civilised.

Judge Wiseman was the inevitable exception; he was offhand to the defendants, but vile to representatives—from either side. I was once trying to discuss an offer of repayment with the opposing solicitor, but all she could fix her mind on was the day's list, and the judge's name stamped next to our hearing.

'Oh God, we've got Wiseman. He's a bastard from hell.' She quavered.

We never agreed on the offer, but we could agree on that. I was astonished how little protection those judges had; we all sat around a table, they had no elevated seat of judgment, they were separated from the rest of us only by a row of law-books, and there were no court staff. I assumed there must be hidden panic-buttons or some such dotted around, but perhaps Judge Renfrew was kept safe by his air of paternal authority, Harlow by her humanity, and the Bastard From Hell by his scary bastardicness.

I was a regular at the County Court during what I at first referred to as the Warrant Flurry, and then the Warrant Storm, intensified. Just like Matty and Eloise, people were struggling on withering incomes and rising costs, and mortgage-payers no longer had the security that their house was worth more than their debt; the arrival of the unthinkable had exposed them to peril that had previously seemed impossible. At the suggestion of Judge Renfrew, we had set up a Court Desk scheme; I squatted in a borrowed office, small chairs and desk wedged between dozing filing cabinets, emerging to haunt the court waiting room to offer help to nervous-looking defendants discreetly pointed my way by Bob the court usher. In the cabinet-store, I could look over their court papers, discuss their finances, offer advice to those missing out on benefits, hammer out a payment offer and find the solicitor for the other side before hasty negotiations and being summoned to the judge's chambers, walking in with unfortunates who thought they faced show-trial, vitriolic allegations, cold condemnation and summary hanging. The palace of the Ice Dragon.

They were surprised to be seated at a table in a book-lined room, with a judge in a suit but no frills or rugs, trying to hammer out a house-saving deal. Things got so busy I would flit between hearings, plunging from one judge's room to another, hearing them ask 'Where's the adviser? Ah, here he comes, at a sprint, sit you down, catch your breath, catch your breath…'

My collar digging in, tie trying to strangle me, heart rate rising, sweating with nervous, hope no one notices fear. And if I feel like this, what about the poor sod next to me? How does it feel to know that in minutes, with no more than a stroke of a pen, you may have to go home to pack, or even won't have a home to return to? *Where will we go? How will my children cope? How will my marriage survive? What will the no-longer neighbours say?* I was no lawyer, I never pretended to be Perry Mason. Perhaps Rumpole of the Bailey once or twice. We were advisers, referred to as 'MacKenzie Friends', we had no rights to be heard in court and strictly should have only hand-held, paper-shuffled, ear-whispered and not attempted to speak; but the judges were pragmatists and realised it would save time to allow us leeway. They knew the defendants' jeopardy, and with the descent upon us of the unthinkable-impossible, the numbers of those puzzled defendants grew.

The judges did what they could, but sometimes had no choice but to award possession of, eviction from, beloved homes. They knew that there were no friendly, welcoming places for the ousted. Council housing stock was depleted as tenants bought their homes, then in so many cases their income stuttered, their mortgages rose and those former tenants, now in-arrears homeowners, found themselves in the court waiting room—*how did we get here, how did this happen?*

Sometimes it went beautifully right. One tenant, mired in arrears, had never claimed Housing Benefit—

nobody had told the family they were entitled, and being made to put pen to paper was the worst torture they could suffer—but with an adjournment granted by Judge Renfrew, a benefit application and useful backdating rules (later slashed to ribbons by government), six months' arrears and an eviction warrant disappeared. Similarly, I sat with a family who had been pinned, helpless, in the face of unpayable costs whose struggle ended when I checked their entitlement to what was then known as Family Credit, and found they were underclaiming by £50.00 every week—a lot of money, life-changing. Sometimes we had to fight and fight again: Mr Michaels' mortgage lender wanted him out, they pressed time and again, serving a fresh warrant every time he fell behind by so much as a penny. In reply to every warrant came my hastily-scribbled applications to suspend. On the fourth or fifth hearing, Judge Renfrew signed off the new terms of payment, waving Mr Michaels out and fixing me with the stare of a wise owl who had spied a mouse. 'I do not wish to see you or this case again, is that understood?'

'Yes, Sir, understood.'

With rent arrears cases, there was a chance, especially if the person lived in council housing, that things could be made to work even if there was no last-minute cleverness to display regarding unclaimed benefits. The judge would check keenly to see how punctually the defendant had paid before they ran into problems—woe betide those whose payments were erratic and unexplained—but all but the truly incorrigible would be offered one last chance. Private rent cases were harder; the landlords fought harder for bigger, faster payments, and sometimes they just wanted the property back, for their own occupation, as the financial jeopardy spread and their property empire dissolved. With mortgages, the curse was the negative equity; even with a good offer of payment, the mortgagee could complain their security was at risk, and a reluctant judge might have to award possession. Even so, at the end of a long battle, when hope was extinguished, the judges tried to allow time, for the defendant to move out, or for them to seek help from the councils Homelessness Team.

'Eviction granted,' ordered Renfrew on too many sad occasions, 'but the warrant is to lie in the office for three weeks. That is all I can do.' The last few words were added, *obiter*.

(vi)

The Council Tax—rates as was, then, briefly, and disastrously, the Poll Tax ('Community Charge' insisted one pedantic snot with whom I attempted to negotiate, 'It is the *Community Charge*.'). If you don't pay you get a court summons. Ignore? You may receive a letter from bailiffs. Ignore, avoid? But eventually someone pops up on your doorstep at some sleep-drenched pre-dawn hour announcing they are 'an officer of the law'. Not so easy to ignore; a warrant is out for your arrest. On the first go, you can attend court 'under your own recognisance'. Ignore that one and they return, this time you go straight to the cells until the bench is ready to hear you. This, possibly, shocked more people than the terse, itsy-bitsy eviction warrant.

The Magistrates' Court was a different, harsher world from the County Court. Where the latter was hidden in an anonymous office building with a modest plaque marking its entrance, the former announced itself in large metallic letters over its large glass doors, a large red-brick building housed close to the police station, with obvious streams of traffic in between. Its forbidding look told lookers-on *we have cells here*. The court rooms were large, too; open, with polished wooden seats for the parties to a case, a public gallery, docks, witness box, and above all, a large, raised dais at which sat three Magistrates—the bench. Unlike the District Judges, I never knew their names, I was never able to attach personalities to them, only to their ever-present Clerk (a sneering, squinting malevolence who rapidly became known to me as Torquemada).

There was little point attempting to soothe the nerves of defendants who came there, as they came through the imposing doors to see ushers in cloaks, solicitors, barristers a-scurry, uniformed security staff who appeared like jailers, police officers in and out. This was the home of a rougher form of justice. The court's power was to examine the debtor under oath as to their means—also, to establish if they had possessed money, what did they do with it if not paying a priority debt such as the Council Tax? People genuinely struggling might get their debts reduced, occasionally wiped out altogether; others may be given a last chance to make a sustainable arrangement. Those, however, who had shown 'wilful refusal' to pay, or who had demonstrated 'culpable neglect' could be on the receiving end of a suspended sentence, or an immediate short spell in prison.

John, the council's officer at these hearings, told me that one smirking cheekychappie had asked the bench, 'What are you gonna do about it eh?'

He got his thirty-day answer.

Unlike the County Court, the Magistrates' Court did not invite us to help those who were struggling, we asked the Court if we could. The request was always considered an intriguing curiosity by the inscrutable bench.

Torquemada did not like amateurs in his court, and revelled in every embarrassment and mistake as we endeavoured to establish a helpful presence, *amicas curiae*. One day, owing to a diary error, I arrived at ten a.m. with a defendant who turned out to be due to be seen at two p.m.: acting as I would with the County Court, I arranged to meet the defendants at the correct time, and left. Not long after I got back to my office, I picked up the phone to hear an acidic voice, 'You should have stayed on the premises, to be seen when we were ready. We'll accept it as an honest mistake this time, and there will be no punishment.' As he finished, I could picture him leering happily.

Prior to trying our first hearings, some colleagues and I attended the Magistrates' sessions as observers. One young man took to the witness box, his gait and bearing combining both a swagger and an incipient cower; it was hard to read what was in his mind. It was put to him by the bench that he had not attempted to make any payments to his Council Tax account for over a year; what reason could he give? He cowered now a little more; shades of the prison-house were falling.

'It's a bit hard…' He chewed his lip.

The bench composed themselves for patience but Torquemada was like a bulldog on the end of its chain, straining, *lemmeaddim*!

'See, I was doing a lot of dope, well, not just dope, other stuff…'

It was not a good start; the bench was turning chilly and a lopside-smiling Torquemada was now like Pierrepoint measuring his man for the drop.

'So anyway I was getting in a mess of debt, and the guys I owed it to, they don't write letters and don't hold courts, know waddi mean? I got so scared, I told a mate what trouble I was in, and he got a loan, I can't get one see, and he paid them off, everything, got them off my back.'

The bench sat, suspended in judgment, as Torquemada scowled silently.

'So, this mate, he comes back to tell me what he's done and that I'm safe…' Everyone present knew there was a 'but' yet to drop. 'But then he gets out his gun and puts it to my head, says now you pay me, or I'll kill you.'

Silence in court.

'So that's why I couldn't pay this bill. I could hardly borrow off him again. Helped me keep off drugs, though…'

'Ah yes,' the bench deadpanned, 'we think we see.' To Torquemada's disgust, the defendant was spared a stretch in the cells.

Just before I attended my first hearings, my fears for the success of this project deepened. My wife was a member of a Tennis Club and, stuffed once again reluctantly into a suit, I went along to a formal dinner; the Club Secretary graced our table, and he was a Magistrate from a nearby area. 'Maybe you'll pick up tips,' said my wife. 'Yes, I see them all,' the legal man held forth, 'I see them all from the inner cities with their curly hair and thick lips and big arses, I see the light-fingers and the fairies, Pikies and Pakis, and… yes, I am racist, sexist and homophobic.' He flashed a warning glare to douse any incipient Political Correctness around the table. 'But once I am in court I do my job, I can set all that aside and I judge everyone fairly.'

We left before the main course arrived, pleading medical reasons.

I wouldn't wish Mr and Mrs Saxon's luck on anyone. An exhausted middle aged couple, they brought in one of the biggest bags I had encountered; they had enormous debts, an income shrivelling like an old balloon, fractious, intractable family problems, poor health and noisy, vindictive neighbours. At the bottom of their bag swam a summons to Means Enquiry for a debt of over £2000; Council Tax. Bailiffs had sent back their warrant having poked around their house and come away empty-handed; *nulla bona*. No Goods. Broke. They had borrowed to pay off old borrowings, which were to pay off older borrowings, loans rolled up until the interest was compound in the manner of a financial fracture. The bullies and shouters piled on; the couple curled up and allowed themselves to be berated and battered—what else could they do?

I wrote up their situation and sent the report to John and to the Magistrates. I accompanied a frightened Mr and Mrs Saxon to court, but as a non-lawyer I could not be heard there, I had to sit with them on the smooth, polished benches, looking up at the raised dais where 'the bench' sat, citizens in judgment of others and Torquemada in judgment of everyone. I was nervous; Mr and Mrs Saxon looked too timid to fight, too drained. John, sympathetic, did his bit and took care not to make the situation worse. The bench read my report with enigmatic, unmoving faces. Mrs Saxon heaved against a Ventolin inhaler, whiffs of spray, whoops of breath that would not come. Still poker-faced, the bench questioned the Saxons; Mrs Saxon leant into the inhaler and stuttered tearfully through her evidence. 'We will rise to consider the facts.' The Chair of Magistrates announced, and they were gone through a small door in a high wall which, despite the dignity of its courtroom crest, looked like a theatre set.

I did what I could to calm and comfort the Saxons, but all the time I thought of the Tennis Secretary. *I hear their stories and I don't believe a one of them. Lying is in their blood, the damn lot of them.'* I chatted briefly to John, who was on the bench in front of ours. The theatre-set door opened once more and the bench took their seats in silence. Mr and Mrs Saxon were bidden to rise.

'We have considered carefully.' the Chair was still shuffling papers, but then looked up, straight at my couple. 'In view of the financial and other circumstances we have decided to remit the sum in its entirety.'.

A long silence dampened the room; Mr and Mrs Saxon, white-faced and uncomprehending, tottered, and she took a sharp last-breath blast from the inhaler.

'That means you do not owe the money anymore. Thank you for attending this hearing, you may go home.'

Mrs Saxon heaved against the inhaler, but this time the momentum carried her downwards; she landed against the polished bench and slid to the floor, gasping for breath that always stayed cruelly-teasing, just inches away. As I was about to call for medical help, John half-turned to me, but instead of speaking uttered a loud, pained cry and he too flopped to the floor.

'We will rise now,' pronounced the bench, and were offstage in moments, leaving me, Torquemada, a jug of water and two recumbent bodies. The chaos abated as quickly as it had descended. Mrs Saxon had collapsed from sheer relief and was now adrenalin-breathing, shaking, but recovering. John had caught himself a sharp blow in the chest from a jutting bit of bench; he was bruised, but on his feet quickly.

Justice was truly done on that day. I sometimes wonder what became of Mr and Mrs Saxon, because only one of their many troubles was laid to rest.

(vii)

Mr Voxey had been running for a long time; perhaps 'running' is not the correct word, 'dodging' would be better, zigzagging, just enough—place to place, time to time—to elude his pursuers. The mistake he made was to assume that every time the hounds were not audibly baying at his heels after a quick change of address, a false trail or two, that he was safe. Those who stalk do not howl; silence is their camouflage.

Picture Mr Voxey in his latest-new-home, relaxing in his chair, breathing easy after some twists and turns, leafing through the parochial trivia of the local press. An advertisement in a little bold box bears his name. He hasn't won the lottery, he isn't being sought by legacy-offering lawyers; his name is on display because he is to be made bankrupt.

The zigzagging is over.

Come out, come out, wherever you are.

Mr Voxey was due to appear at The Appropriate County Court at 2pm on The Stated Date. He could continue to hide, but that wouldn't stop him being empty-chaired and made bankrupt anyway. He came to see me with his bagful of papers, the story of a failed trader who took to his heels in fear and incomprehension, with the cutting of the advert as a terse last chapter. Mr Voxey had nothing, no money, no property; he was ill, he would never work again. His creditors hadn't sought his bankruptcy because they believed he would be forced to surrender a hidden pot of gold or even a measly pension fund, they were simply fed up and had decided to punish him.

I put on my suit, Mr Voxey donned his faded best, and we turned up at the County Court. On the waiting toom wall, a typed notice advised 'District Judge Cheyne is to be addressed as "Madam" in court.' Some wag had pencilled 'Call Me Madam' at the bottom of the blue paper. We waited; we were called.

Madam was a severe-looking middle aged woman who wore no makeup apart from a dying-ember glow of lipstick; this patch of light didn't humanise her but made her look even more formidable. Mr Voxey was ordered to sit, and he flopped into place, strings cut. After I sat, I was asked who did I think I was and what did I think I was doing there? I explained that Mr Voxey was an exhausted dodger who hadn't understood the gravity of what faced him, but now he did and he 'wishes to show due respect to the court'.

'Oh. Good.' The possibility of some new zigzag being dismissed from her mind, Madam set to work, ensuring all the correct papers had been issued at the correct times; a few pen-flicks later and it was done.

'Bankrupt at—2.15pm.'

Mr Voxey appeared braced for the cold clasp of the

derbies and the rough hand of the jailer on his shoulder; instead, Madam waved us away, warning the bankrupt that his next appointment would be with the Official Receiver, a humourless official who dealt harshly with zigzaggers. He was not going to run again. It was over.

(viii)

A cheese salad roll, a bag of crisps, a chocolate bar; my usual lunch. Weight gain, courtesy of Purchasing Power and lack of willpower. The sun was dazzling me close-eyed as I crossed the chessboard flags of the market square, and I heard-felt the heavy thudding footsteps as someone pelted up behind me; a hand fell on to my shoulder and I swung, holding out my lunch-bag on the urging of an odd instinct—defence or appeasement?

Relief—it was a friend; hands now on his knees, bent, breathless, but a friend, from the council's benefits office.

'Glad I caught you.' he wheezed, waving me to wait-wait, catching breath. 'Need a word.' Another fill of air. 'You've got someone today, two o'clock appointment: don't see him, dangerous, he's in on a very complex fraud, he owns his home but he's claiming help with rent—he's not renting. We're investigating. Steer clear of him.'

His breath was not quite back when we parted company and I sauntered back to the office, bemused. What fraudster would consult us? A quick look at the papers and then: 'Sorry, that's fraud, we can't represent you'.

My 2pm had the wary look of a man who had been landed too many hefty blows over a long lifetime, someone whose dignity, his last possession, was under final siege. When he was born, his home had been in India; he was a youngster when it became part of Pakistan. He had come to the UK with an entrepreneur's conviction that its people would adore ghee sweets—and was now suffering a pensioner's regrets. He too wheezed, but no amount of breath-catching would help, and although he could make himself understood in English, his sentences had a stop-go quality, halting and fading as if he expected any moment to be interrupted with loud shouting. Was this man naught but a cunning fraudster, out to gull and bind me to his plan?

His dream of a ghee empire had turned out not to be so sweet, he had struggled on, but now he had to sacrifice his pride, he had a mortgage to pay and was running out of money. He had enquired, he had been pointed to the Housing Benefit office, he was given a form and filled it in as instructed. At no time had anyone told him Housing Benefit was for rent only. All he knew was that he needed help. A phone call was all it took to resolve the matter and apply for the correct benefit. As a fraud, it was all a bit of a dud; as for the alleged complexity... But what would have happened to him had I done as I was bid, and shut my door to him?

The voice of the Ice Dragon whispered, *they're all at it, it's all fraudulent...* pub and neighbour-chats all said the same, fuelled by tabloid headlines. I never saw one genuine fraudster in the years I was there; as I say, why would they come near people who would call them for what they were? Occasionally I saw victims of fraud, harmed by the sideswipes of someone else's petty, desperate cupidity. Mrs Vosper was a disabled pensioner who came to see me when her weekly money was cut by the then-vast sum of £40; there had been no change in her circumstances, no new money, no sudden wealth or unexpected late marriage. Unable to work out why her money should fall so sharply, I picked up the phone to the Benefits Agency, the rebadged DHSS, at that time an informed and helpful organisation, though heading downhill apace.

'It's her son—he's claimed an allowance as her carer. That cuts her money—in effect the £40 a week transfers to him.'

Ah.

A few questions.

–Does your son come to see you much?

–No. Once a month at best, and only then when he's pestering for money and I've got none. He hates me and I hate him.

–Ah. So he couldn't really be described as your carer?

–Yer kidding. He only cares about himself.

–So… he doesn't spend at least thirty-five hours a week looking after you, helping with your health and mobility problems?

–Are you having a laugh?

I called the Benefits Agency back, and mother threw son to the wolves.

'Teach him a bloody lesson,' she said, gathering her things with satisfaction.

Mrs Jantry's husband owed money to a business associate, who had thrived as Mr Jantry failed. When it became clear that the Jantrys were willing but unable to pay, Mr Jantry's one-time friend sued and, owing to their failure to reply to his court action, won an Order that they should pay the debt 'forthwith'. This didn't change their finances, and so the creditor turned DIY debt collector; he decided to visit the Jantrys, to 'reason with them', but also to find out if they were living in a mansion while holding back his few-thousand pounds. It was on their modest council doorstep that, for the first time, he saw Mrs Jantry, and within a moment his heart melted. He was stunned, stricken, and money mattered no longer. I will forget the debt, he told Mr Jantry, but I want one thing: *her*.

Appalled at bargaining over human collateral, the Jantrys gave their answer, forbade return visits, and so the DIY debt collector withdrew to brood on his wrongs and work out how to gain his prize. He became a self-taught expert in the County Court Green Book, and in the dense ranks of rules in its hundreds of pages, found and used a procedure that Fairway Collections had toyed with, as a spurious threat; he had an unpaid debt and he could apply for the debtor to be required to attend court to be examined under oath as to their income and assets. Refusal to attend could be punished as contempt of court. The proceedings were meant to help a creditor decide the form of enforcement to get their debt paid most effectively, but for the DIY Debt Collector it had an additional, delicious beauty; it would force her to be there, with him. It was a way to see her, talk to her, press his suit in more than one sense, for a precious, legally sanctioned tryst.

Baffled, Mr and Mrs Jantry attended court, filled out a long questionnaire with brief answers (Income—Unemployment Benefit—Capital held—Nil—Other Assets—Nil), took their oaths, politely answered the polite questioning of the District Judge, then submitted to a series of pointless questions from the DIY Debt Collector, during which he gazed at nothing and no one but Mrs Jantry, except once at the Judge, as if to say 'Give me—Order it.' The parties went away from the courtroom, the Jantrys could not pay—and by this time the DIY did not *want* them to; he wanted the debt to remain forever, so as often as possible he could pay his fee, make the date, command their, *no*, her, presence, and dream of happiness in open court.

This love story ended, not with syrupy strings, a quiet consumptive cough and a kiss goodbye, nor some miraculous realignment of affections, nor even the convenient death of an inconvenient husband followed by comfort-cooing to a grieving widow. Whatever was lurking within the twisted 'millsyboonsy' imagination of the DIY Collector, it was perceived and put out of its misery by the perspicacious Judge Harlow. 'This hearing, and from what I can see, its predecessors, has no practical or legal function,' she pronounced. 'There will be no further applications for Oral Examination without prior permission of the court.'

I had never seen a man's lights go out before—though I had felt the sensation in my own breast a few times—and the slump of shoulders of someone who, once-powerful, at least in his own mind, was now drained, limp. Mr and Mrs Jantry were grateful to the Judge, who asked Bob the usher to mind them in the waiting room while his colleague, Jim, made sure the DIY Collector had left the premises. I said goodbye to Mr and Mrs Jantry and returned to my office, musing.

Should I have sympathised with the DIY in any way? No, certainly not: he had abused the system, he was a stalker with a grudge, too much money and a few legal forms. It took me a while to work out what pathetic fellow-feeling existed between us: 'White Arrow—Blue Background'. Now *that* felt uncomfortable.

Then there was Tarquin: he bore the name of a tyrant, a ravisher, but the guileless face of a small boy lost in the school corridors, fretting about missing lessons. He became the only person I knew to eject himself from the entire benefits system through guilelessness, left to live on imaginary money. To see he was a misfit required only a passing read of his face; that he had been bullied in his school days was a hat-eating certainty. Quietly singsong spoken, gentle, a here-not-here light from his eyes, he was not fully connected to this Earth. He was out of work; had never worked.

At some point, an unknown relative had given up the ghost and left Tarquin the sum of £25,000: it is relevant to point out at this time that capital of over

£8000 was sufficient to stop Tarquin's benefits altogether.

So: did he seek advice about the legacy?

No. He had a dream, and this windfall was its consummation.

He closed his claims and went abroad.

For three months.

To a sequence of movie theme parks.

And, £25,000 later, he returned, reclaiming his benefits as if nothing had happened. Sorry, they said, you can't have this benefit, you've got too much in the bank. But I haven't, he replied, hurt; literally not a penny. Literally has nothing to do with it, said the powers that be, you have £25000 to live on, whether it's there or not. So live on it. Tarquin consulted a solicitor, who challenged the decision—and lost.

Tarquin ended up in my office because nobody knew what to do; still no job, still no benefits, and only imaginary money in the bank. He was surviving on food parcels from a charity, but nobody could stop his rent spiralling out of control, they too had a notion that he had money in the bank. I'm afraid I didn't know what to do either: it was too late to reopen the appeal, the benefits decisions were correct in law anyway, nobody wanted to employ Tarquin and his landlord became increasingly keen on evicting him. When Tarquin was seen in the town calmly and systematically sorting through one waste bin after another, I got his permission to contact his doctor—and unusually my letter was rewarded with a direct phone call.

'I know what you're trying to do—get him a

disability benefit that isn't affected by that money. I wish I could help, but you see Tarquin is not ill or disabled in any way. I have known him all his life, he is *bizarre.* And as far as I know there is no Bizarreness Benefit, is there?'

No: indeed. But damndamndamn, if only this had been told to the solicitor who appealed Tarquin's case: there was a possible winning argument here. Tarquin had taken and spent that money in the way that he did because it never occurred to him to behave in any other way. He acted as he would always have acted, without calculation, without any notion of the consequences. He lost the lot as a bizarreness disbenefit. He had innocented himself out of the entire benefits system.

One last try: I explained that all avenues were closed, and that getting a job of some sort was the one-and-only. 'Is there anything we can help you with, applying for training, government schemes, anything?'

His lost-in-corridor look reappeared.

'Is there any kind of job you're especially interested in?'

After a long pause he said, 'I would like to...'

'Yes?'

'I would like to be... a film star.'

My eyes wandered to my office window, but it didn't open far enough for me to jump.

That discussion was the last note I made on Tarquin's case, in that job. I didn't move on because of him; warning signs, but of another sort, had been apparent for a long time. The faction who did not want to 'celebrate deprivation' any longer had caucused its way to political power and purse-strings holding, and I pictured myself emptying my desk, packing boxes and going back to the queue for the giro, unless I cleared out pronto.

I didn't want to be a film star.

I yearned to be a writer.

Who was I to criticise unrealistic ambitions?

The Old King With A Foot In The Door

Bailiffs.

What are they?
 Who commissions and controls them?
 When can they descend on you? The middle of the night?
 Do you have to let them in?
 Can they break into your house?
 Can they put a foot in your door?
 Can they march you off to a cell?
 What's the difference between a bailiff and a debt collector?

Admit it: you don't know. To be fair, hardly anyone does, bailiffs included. Not even lawyers know it all. The nearest I ever met to a sage on the subject was The Expert, and he would probably admit modestly there are limits to his knowledge, too. He comes in later.
 In the latter part of the bright t-shirt years, bailiffs of a particular sort became very active—sent by the local council to visit its impoverished citizens to recover local taxes; amid the warrant-storm of repossessions and the confusion caused by the red-letter shouters, the local authority decided to assert its primacy as a creditor.

Bailiffs were one of a number of options they could use to recover money—another was the frightening Means Enquiry that gave Mr and Mrs Saxon their dramatic day in court. And these were real bailiffs, proper ones, not chancers exploiting debtors' fears, not lineshooters hoping to grab quick money. Private firms but deemed 'fit and proper persons' to undertake a deadly-serious business.

Bailiffs: the word sparked fear of humiliation, public exposure, shame, of the stocks, medieval splatterings.

What goods can they take?
    What goods *can't* they take?
    Can they take away your car?
    Can they look through a window and say that's enough, they've seized all the goods they've seen?
    I've heard they can't take anything that's in use: quick, switch everything *on!*

In one case years ago, a woman in Liverpool was returning from buying milk. Bottle in hand, she opened her front door and stepped inside, just as a man rushed in behind her, forcing his way into the property. Thinking all sorts of horrors had descended on her, the woman swung round, lashed out—milk bottle in hand. The person she laid out was a bailiff, who took her to court on a charge of assault.
    Was she found guilty?

The problem here is 'years ago'; once again, the cold, clinging grasp of the past. We're not going back as far as the Latinate solidus and denarius that lasted so long, but we are time travelling again.

So: when bailiff law was first codified in England, who was King?

Canute, that's who.

No tide jokes, please.

At that time, the seizure of goods by bailiffs—'distress', what an all-round applicable word—concerned cattle. Can't pay? We'll impound your cows. If you take them back without paying, that's poundbreach. Or is it *rescous*? If there are no goods, the bailiffs can return the warrant, *nulla bonna*. One thing is for sure, King Canute never envisaged bailiffs coming along to seize cars, tellies and games consoles, but by the 1990s, the same laws applied, with a little tinkering here and there as history pottered along. Part of the problem was that unlike livestock, shiny modern consumer goods don't hold their value, and once taken and auctioned they fetched negligible sums, and so in most cases the debt was barely diminished even when a house was emptied.

Can they squat in your house until their mates come to take your furniture away?

If you sign an agreement to pay, but they have listed 'seized' goods, who owns those goods?

If a bailiff lies to you as a subterfuge to get into your home, is that legal? Can they just laugh in your face and commence seizing?

It was 1993; let's say it was, I can't recall precisely, but I do know it was a long time since Canute ruled the waves. I picked up a call from an agitated householder with an unwelcome visitor. What followed was like listening to a mind's-eye drama, a radio play, with me left sidelined, unable to help.

'She's in my house, *in my house!*'

'Who is?'

'She said she was from the council! She said could she come in, have a quiet word about my debt—less embarrassing, so the neighbours can't hear!'

Oh dear.

'So she comes in, immediately says she's a bailiff and she's going to take my stuff away! She lied to me! Can you stop her?'

'I'll speak to her.'

'Come here and talk to the adviser.' I heard the enraged householder prompt the bailiff.

Noises off-mike—muffled, but undeniable and undeniably arrogant, refusal.

'*Talk to him!* What's wrong with you?'

Further noises off.

'She says if I try to stop her, she'll call the police and have me arrested! Can she do that?'

'Not to help her take goods away—only to prevent a breach of the—'

'Sod this, I'm phoning the coppers myself!'

It took a while to find out what followed: the police did attend, and one of the two women was arrested and removed in handcuffs. Yes; the bailiff. Officers attending the premises had encountered an angry, abusive individual who proceeded to threaten them when they questioned the legality of her actions. To the station…

Kerfuffle then followed: the bailiff company, aghast and enraged, threatened legal action against all concerned, eventually entering proceedings against the police; 'Just wait till we get this into court!' That's what I said, the council officers too.

Who was in the right? What would happen? At least our householder didn't sock the bailiff with a milk bottle. Coming back to which, the bailiff's claim in that case was unsuccessful; what self-respecting householder with a man rushing her from behind wouldn't think that the worst was happening, and react accordingly? But what was the answer in this case? It was time to turn to The Expert.

I had attended training courses run by The Expert; I wanted to be a trainer and I wanted to model myself on his easy, informed style. But anyway; I telephoned him, and he was very interested.

'There is a precedent—it's from 1648.'

More recent than Canute, but still dizzyingly remote. A court found that a bailiff who had misrepresented what he was to gain access to the debtor's premises had not gained entry or seized goods legally.

We were going to win.

A little later, however, there was a return call from The Expert. 'Sorry, there's a later case—1677, came to the opposite conclusion and it trumps the earlier one.'

We were going to lose.

Which part of the remote past would govern events of the present day?

But there never was any court hearing. In keeping with the zeitgeist, the bailiff company encountered its own financial problems; it went out of business.

I wonder… if they sent bailiffs to the bailiffs?

Someone Has To Pay

Clean, bright, smart, glowing, the café was how you want the future to be. I've never liked the taste of coffee, but the whirring of the grinder, the steam and heat, the bowl-like cups, glinting glasses and polished counter all attracted me, gave me an odd, wild optimism. It was a small place, a welcoming, comfortable recess in an indoor arcade closed in behind spotless glass doors: what we have here, whispered its friendly ambience, is a place to relax.

But I was not relaxed. I shifted and shuffled in my chair, I turned the small laminated one-page menu over and over in my hands without looking at its cheerful-font offerings. Was she going to come? She wasn't, was she? I suffered the needle-point agony of the stood up, but I could never say that, we were not dating, is that clear? I hung on in hope, wanting to avoid the humiliation of ordering and leaving alone. The door swung open with a sound like an intake of breath, a sigh, and I looked up too quickly, too hopefully. A couple hand-held their way to the next table and sat, chatting. I turned the menu over and over. If-when she comes I'll buy lunch, I'll pay, I'll insist, as a friend, a good friend, not to create obligation, no.

My stomach knotted tighter, tighter. Not coming. And I would never be able to ask why. But I was not stood up, this was just a friend who was too busy to make it, understand? There was more grinding, more bursts of steam, I tried to remember when I first decided I didn't like coffee, when I finally gave up sugar, whether the teas on the plasticised menu would taste like tea or if they would be insipid hot water with the taste of pencil shavings. Perhaps I should try that lovely-smelling fresh coffee, surely it was worlds better than the dreadful powder of my childhood. Still not there. I didn't order, that would have been rude, defeatist. I had to wait. For her.

She arrived on a cold breeze that fought against being shut out. The café's warmth regained the upper hand as she sat. Don't say thanks for coming. Don't ask what held her up. Just be glad. I handed her the pawed-over menu.

'Give me a minute, can't you?'

I looked at the knot-swirls on the table top.

'Been here long?'

Nonono, course not.

'I haven't got long. Work.' Oh. A breakup-tense silence settled on us; both had look-away eyes. Yes there is a breakup, I wanted to tell the next table, but it wasn't us, not me anyway, and it wasn't her fault, boyfriend had his midlife crisis at thirty, cheated, lied, bastard, eh? She's rebuilding, I'm helping, I just want to be a good friend, and... I stopped explaining, confiding, they couldn't hear and wouldn't have listened.

'I don't want much. Not hungry. Don't let that stop you.' She set down the menu.

Two cheese toasties, two Americanos, it was an echo-order. I regretted the coffee, modern-day wasn't better than old. Conversation dragged painfully. She'd got a flatmate. A man, yes, but just to split the bills. Oh and she was applying for a new job, new town, new start. Good idea, great idea, yeah. I dropped strings of melted cheese down my shirt. Her laugh was another cold breeze.

'I have to go.' It seemed seconds since 'I haven't got long…' Best not ask her to stay, she had abandoned her food and half her coffee.

'I'll get the bill. My treat.'

'I wouldn't have come otherwise.'

That was her goodbye. I stood up at that clean, polished counter, paid and wound the receipt around my finger in what I hoped was a casual, confident gesture. I left as unhurriedly as I could.

The Caring Bank

'He that is down may fear no fall' (Bunyan)

> **IMPORTANT—**
> **YOU SHOULD READ THIS CAREFULLY**
>
> **Default Notice** under Section 87(1) of The Consumer Credit Act 1974
> Agreement No, 05141373 Personal Loan agreement between The Customer and The Caring Bank dated 5/5/2006.
> You are in breach of this Agreement to the extent of £3000. You have 14 days to remedy the breach etcetera etcetera etcetera ohbloodyhell

Thank you for calling The Caring Bank. Your call is in a queue. Thank you for your patience. Your call is important to us. Thank you for calling The Caring Bank...

Sigh.

People say if you press 0 when you're stuck in the soup of an automated menu, you get straight through to a person. It doesn't work. Nor does sighing. Or swearing. Or insulting the sci-fi hold voice.

Your call is important to us.

Default Notice
Sigh.

'Now, it's nothing to panic about,' the adviser in the bright t-shirt would say, 'but we don't ignore it either. It's calling in a debt, but they can't go to court for their money until they've issued this, and as you'll see it gives you time to contact them to discuss it, make an offer of payment, and it even tells you to seek advice. It's as much a protection for you as it as a debt notice for them.'

But I wasn't listening to the adviser in the bright t-shirt. He was gone, dumped into the past, I no longer had his breeze, his courage, his business-like confidence.

Thank you for calling The Caring Bank. Your call is in a queue. Thank you for your patience. Your call is important to us. Thank you for calling The Caring Bank…

Important to me, too. I was shuddering-nervous, the phone jiggled in my hand.

Default Notice

Someone with a fine, cruel sense of irony had served a Section 87 Notice on me. On *me*.

Your call is important to us.

I wondered what it would be like.

In bright t-shirt days, I'd made hundreds of calls; discussed, debated, argued, negotiated. One time an HP company called me; a hornet voice buzzing venom at the other end of the line.

'So: you want us not to repossess the car, *Sir*. But you can't pay the instalments, *Sir*. You have yet to pay one third of the instalments, *Sir*, so we don't even have to go to court for permission. You can't stop us, *Sir*.'

'Could I just—'

'We're not interested in your excuses, *Sir*, we are going to come and take the vehicle.'

'Could I just—'

'And don't try hiding the car, *Sir*, that would not be the least bit clever. It is *our* car.'

'Could I just—'

'What makes you, *Sir*, think you are so special that you can keep *our* car without paying for it? What makes you so different from other people, *Sir*?'

'Could I just—' I started laughing, I couldn't help it.

'I don't think there is anything funny about this situation, *Sir*, I suggest you start taking things seriously.'

'You… you've got your numbers mixed up,' my words were staggered by giggles. 'I'm not your customer, I'm the debt adviser who wrote to you.'

The venom-voice choked.

'Yep, you've got the wrong person, put on the wrong persona. Still, you've given me a fascinating insight into your customer service standards, thank you.'

Phoneslam, line cut—*ooooooooooooooooooooooooooooo*.

But The Caring Bank had got the right number, the right customer.

Your call is important to us.

Sigh.

Can't be. Never! It is. It cannot be. What are the odds—

It's her, surely it's her. That voice, that tone, that

attitude, the way she used my name, stripped of any title, to intimidate, humiliate, infantilise: as a *sting*.

'Could I speak to the person I spoke to last time? It would save so much unnecessary explanation.'

'That is not how our system works, *stingname*.'

'But surely the last person took notes? Surely you can pick up from there rather than drag me through the whole dratted routine—'

'That is not how our system works, *stingname*.'

'Look, I keep on having the same conversation with The Caring Bank, and it isn't helping. I have no money with which to pay you, read the notes, read my letters to you. When I took out the loan I was working, earning well. Now I'm not. Everything's changed. Read the notes.'

'That is not my problem, *stingname*. You owe this bank three thousand pounds.'

'Look at the notes. Look up my payment record. Paid in full, every month, until—'

'Until you stopped.'

How she revelled in that petty triumph. How I hated her.

'You should be fully aware of the reason I stopped. It will be in the notes.'

'You need to pay us, *stingname*.'

'Look. At. The. Notes. I have no money, I am not working, I am too ill to work. The more pressure you put on me, the less likely I am to recover.'

'You should have taken out our payment protection insurance, *stingname*.'

'I was self-employed, not eligible for your stupid

loan insurance. I'm too ill to work. I have no income to offer you payment.'

Sigh.

As McLennan once said, it was like beating your head against a sponge.

'If you don't pay we will sue you in the County Court, *stingname*. We can send bailiffs to take your goods away.'

'No you can't.'

'I think you'll find, *stingname*…'

'No. You. Can't.'

'Perhaps you should speak to a debt adviser, *stingname*.'

'I am a debt adviser. Was. That's how I know you can't do what you threaten. You can get a Judgment against me, but the court won't order me to pay what I can't afford. And the court decides, not you. And you can only get a bailiff warrant if I don't pay on the Order.'

'I think you're mistaken, *stingname*.'

'Look. At. The. Notes. You can see what I used to do. You can also see that I'm in the middle of a nasty divorce and my house is for sale. That's why I'm too ill to work. That's why I didn't want to get dragged through all this again. Your "caring" bank will be paid in full once the sale goes through and the money's divided up. I am asking you, for the twentieth time, to back off, suspend action, wait until there is money.'

'It's easy to make promises, *stingname*.'

'Why can you not, not one of you, listen to me?'

'*Stingname*, you owe the Caring Bank three thousand—'

'*Caring* Bank!' I delivered my own sting, downed the receiver.

ooooooooooooooooooooooooooooooooooooooooooooooooooooooooo

E

A railway ticket provides everything a receipt should; solid proof of purchase, symbol, purveyor, displayer of rights, bestower of authority, ownership. Sense of purpose too, because for once in an uncertain world we have a clear statement of where and when we are going, the future foretold and secured by a palm-sized piece of card. We rely on that card, tuck it away somewhere safe, take it out again to make sure it's still there, tuck it away again, look again to make sure it's the right one, not an old one we've neglected to throw away, put it back, pull it out again to recheck the date and time, put it back, pull it out again to make sure the Outward and Return parts are both still there. It is reassurance for our ever-neurotic nature.

On arrival at the station that ticket is a confidence-booster, a statement, a pass, legitimisation, no intruder I, a *bona fide* passenger no less. Show it to a member of staff, slip it into a machine, turnstiles click, we are welcome. Take a seat, make sure it's the right one, hope nobody has taken the booked seat (what to do if they have?), put the tickets away, pull them out again to check those seat details, departure time, is this the correct day? Check them again when the announcement comes that some tickets are not valid on this route. Await departure, hope we're not late, listen to the intensely irritating 'See It Say It Sorted' announcement, eye the aisle, hope no one blocks it with their luggage, hope the catering trolley isn't rolled in just as we reach our station, blocking the exit, excuse-me-excuse-me. Hope we don't need the loo, or at least there is no queue and the loo isn't a disgrace, or occupied for ages by someone who's probably fare-dodging. Hope we get off at the correct station stop, there's never anyone around to ask when you need them and the announcements are inaudible apart from the bing-bong annoying ones about what's available in the shop.

'Tickets Please!' (These days it's 'All tickets and passes please' but let's keep it snappy.) On leaving the train, clutch the Outward portion in hand, not the return, keep that safe. If we put the wrong portion into the machine, would it chew it up or spit it out? Go through the barrier; pull out the Return portion. Return it to safety. The future is assured.

E-ticket, QR code. A whole new language to learn. A little square filled with dots and spots, do you stare at it to see a picture form? Is it a personality test? Do I print it? If I do, what next? Wave it at someone on the gates, show it to a machine, feed it into a slot? Stand and look nonplussed and helpless until someone takes pity? Oh why couldn't they just give me a *ticket?*

The old days were better; you knew where you were. A man would come on to the train and shout out the station's name, with 'All Change!' added if it were needed. In my great-grandad's day, you knew you'd arrived at Longport station because the little chap with a flag would open the door and shout '*Ho-ho-ho-hop out yer buggers!*

I'm in the future, and I'm not comfortable.

'Tickets and passes please!'

I reached into my breast pocket, where my tickets feel safest; cold moment—nothing. Ah, for the twentieth time, there is no cardboard slip, the ticket is 'E', sent to my phone.

Phone out of pocket, phone on. Enter PIN. Can't find the E; it was hell to download, I'd never done such a thing before. It's a generational thing, the kids think nothing of it. Found it. Dates, times, price, it was all there. But did I show that bit to Tickets Please, or the abstract artwork on the other page, if you can call it a page, the black/white oblong with the incomprehensible square spirals? Check the battery level—what if it goes before Tickets Please gets here? Have I brought a charger? Can I use it here, or do a sneaky recharge where I'm going? What if the information was faded or gone, my phone and the machine waved by Tickets Please don't click, marry, beep? How could I prove I was there by rights? The E was sent to me by the venue where I was due to speak; why couldn't they have sent me two little pieces of cardboard? Would Tickets Please call them to verify my story, or just charge me the inflated single fare, or put me off at the next stop? What would I say to the people who'd sent the E?

I hate people who mess with their phones during

meetings. Rude. They should have them confiscated. During the meeting I made surreptitious checks on the battery level and E. Don't fade, please. When I was called on to speak, the pestering, werreting thoughts had to be forced down. I had to concentrate, maintain my train of... oh bloody hell.

Do I delete the E when I get back home? Or just leave it? Does it fade?

I left the meeting checking my phone, looking like a busy man looking up his next thing-to-do: but it was the ticket, the ticket, the wretched E.

Through the barriers.

No one in my seat.

Pull away from platform.

Keep that trolley out of my way; tea please. No, a beer. Ta.

'Tickets and passes please!'

Home at last.

'Ho-ho-ho-hop out yer buggers!'

At the Folly with Life and Soul

Castles, I remember from my childhood *Awake! To History* books, are built on high tops, crags, and unassailable heights. They are grey, grim, with a moat and portcullis to put off callers—add a hail of arrows to drive home the point. Anyone who falls off the dizzying ramparts, that's the end of them. Whoever built the Dunberry Castle was a model-village maker by comparison, that or just a joker. It stood in flat, open ground, approached by a broad, welcoming driveway, the only barrier to the incomer a five-bar gate that swayed easily inwards at the approach of any vehicle. A tumble from Dunberry's pinkish stone walls would result in a soft landing and mild swearing. The place was barely touched by time; it had never seen battle, and no distressed oubliette spectres fretted within. It was pretty, though, and its banqueting hall was ideal for thirty guests at a key-to-the-door dinner. The table was guarded at a respectful distance by suits of armour, polished-up junkyard acquisitions, as were their dulled, blunted swords; the past was not so much presented as parodied, in the spirit of Folly.

Parties are best when guests are already acquainted; we're spared so much awkwardness, we already know who to greet, who to sidle away from, and at this sort of celebration everyone is on their best behaviour, duty bound to a good time. My partner and I had paid for tray-drinks to be offered as people arrived, and for there to be a bottle of wine for every two places at the table; after that it was buy your own, we're not made of money. This party started well; the castle, absent dungeons and clanking chains, had a civilised ambience about it, to feast, chatter and dance its purpose, its being.

Everyone was happy, couples relearned wanting to be with one another, one first date turned into a firm romance and not a few quarrels were patched with bright smiles. On top of this we needed no more, but for all that we met Life and Soul. He was a once-removed relative, but he got on with everyone. He had a share-me smile, he wasn't with anyone, but it was clear that was purely temporary; he delivered DJ patter in a sincere tone, picked up broken-off conversations as if they had been interrupted by a door-knock and not months of silence, glittered with money and had earned every penny; I should have loathed him but, as always, found I could not. Moreover, he demonstrated good taste and generosity: not yet forty, his palate was mature and expert. He swirled the table-wine, appraising critically, tastefully.

'How much did you shell out for this? You were robbed.'

No offence—it was impossible. With an imperious but friendly wave he summoned something better, pronouncing its acute-grave name with brio.

Six clear-glass bottles arrived, pronto: neither red nor white, they caught up the chandelier glow and shone in imitation of the cerise walls. A freshly-opened bottle is a wonderful thing but soon loses its gloss as the first glasses are poured, the line goes down and it is gone, like hope. I saw nothing but the colour of that wine, but I took a generous view and hoped everyone enjoyed it as Life and Soul toured the table, mingling, playing sommelier. Life and Soul was the only person to have the attention of the whole table as he told a joke about a bloke named Dave who claimed he knew everyone; the punchline involved the Pope and should have been obvious, but he bamboozled us expertly for his laugh. Like most party spirits he didn't stand for protracted farewells. He left a comradely miasma behind, and everyone looked forward to the next do, his next showing. The party tottered on for only an hour or so after his departure.

After the last goodnights I went to collect my jacket and thank the staff. I was met with lowered, embarrassed eyes and a muttered explanation that someone had ordered quite a lot of wine but hadn't paid, could I…

I followed the team leader out of the banqueting hall down an armoured walkway; there, and through a string of half-lit corridors with dark, looming offshoots, I had my first impression of castle walls, the dungeon, the oubliette. I was left on the threshold of an empty bar presided over by a tuxedoed manager over whose head, fixed to the wall, swept a scimitar; the first real weapon of destruction I had seen there; a head-lopper, a steely-cold score-settler. I couldn't hold back a joke about the obvious fate of non-payers, but bit my tongue at the urge to explain it wasn't me, honest.

I shelled out a hundred pounds and reeled back down the half-lit corridors to find my partner. She has kept a photo from that late-evening, the two of us posing, happily the worse for wear, my expression a little crooked, stunned, just after Life and Soul had departed.

I kept the receipt, to remind me of that smile, and in the faint hope of a refund.

Traitor's Cash-Out

There was no receipt, no slip; just like the e-ticket on the train, my proof was on a phone screen, and it wasn't even my phone but that of Naughty Pierre. He understood odds; I did not (*two and two is twenty-four…*) and he had placed my bet for me. He worked at a bookie's, constantly risking the sack for his frank advice to punters.

'Hey P, I'm on a streak, won fifty quid, what should I bet on next?'

'Nothing, stop gambling. This is as good as it will get for you.'

'Hey P, nothing's going right, what do I do to make up my losses?'

'Stop gambling, go home.'

So: we were 1-0 up (very early penalty) but playing, *ahem*, unconvincingly: then Iceland equalised within minutes, Sigurdsson connecting with a long throw. At twenty minutes, another long throw, a low shot: the goalie got a hand to it and yet the ball trickled across the line.

We were losing. England. Losing. We were losing but I was winning.

Half Time: 1-2 down. There was pundit-talk of

dropping our goalie for the next game. Naughty Pierre opined that every single last defender needed to be dropped too. And everyone else.

The second half did not encourage us.

At 58 minutes, the online paper reported: *England are embarrassing themselves here. Their movement is ponderous and predictable and if anything, their performance in this second half is even worse than the shift they put in before the interval.*

Pierre and I watched my winnings grow. A tenner stake had risen to fifty pounds.

'Wanna cash out yet?'

All it would take was a push of a button. 'No, we'll see this through.'

My bet was that we would lose. England would lose.

There was still time, there could still be a miracle; I could lose my bet, plus salve my conscience.

If one is English and of a certain age, one must admit to living with a degree of disappointment—I was too young to remember the World Cup victory of 1966 but old enough to remember what came after. England's glory in that legendary match—yes it *was* a goal, you have to go with the ref's ruling, so shut up—brought with it the clinging curse: well done boys, you've done it once, now we expect you to do it again and again and again. That or retreat into refusal to play other countries because we are the best, as happened in early days before we came out to face the world and got a few shocks—Puskas, for instance, or losing 1-0 to the USA in the 1950 tournament. But the presence of the Jules Rimet trophy in our national cabinet eliminated those embarrassments, did it not? Some parts of the past may be safely disposed, to be never mentioned; the better ones may be buffed up, puffed up and stitched with a tapestry touch into our island story.

The first I knew of internationals was 1970, the next World Cup: I was seven years old, I had faith: England were unbeatable and the trophy would shimmer in our hands once more. Why did anyone else even bother turning up? I collected football cards, stuck them in an album; I can still smell the glue, the past clinging, and can remember odd names; Siegfried Held, Bo Larsson. Excited despite the inevitability of victory, I watched rapt: we got to the quarter-finals, against Germany. We won before so we'll do it again, easy-easy. My memory is hazy, but I recall a goalmouth scramble, Sepp Meyer looking desperate as the ball bobbled beyond the reach of his oversized gloves, the commentator bellowing *'The Germans are in all sorts of trouble!'*

Followed by the unthinkable-unpondered. We lost. We. England. People said the shock of that result was enough to turn the General Election. The nation needed new management. It was to become a pattern.

Reel time forward. 1973. The Polish goalie was a clown, Cloughie said so, we were going to win, qualify for another World Cup, be done with past shame: but we didn't. Childhood's tears rolled again, incomprehension, frustration, rage. Pride and patriotism dented. The manager got the sack; it was all his fault. England's winning ways would return.

And so it seemed: Timereel to 1975—not only did we put five goals past Cyprus *(easy-easy!)* but also

Scotland *(yeahhh!)*; I flew my national pride with my newly-bought silky England scarf in the window of a tourist coach as we passed through Glasgow. Not, with hindsight, a very wise thing to do.

Things stalled. Promised 'a hatful of goals' against a team of amateurs from a country smaller than Greater London, we managed a drained, anaemic 1-1 draw. We failed to qualify for the Euro 1976 championship.

Timereel—1977. Scotland had its revenge at Wembley—victory and pitch invasion, tartan fans tearing down goalposts. My pride and patriotism spiralled.

We shed another manager along the way.

Do we have to go to the miseries of 1978? Timereel on, I beg you.

In the late 70s and earliest 80s, my mates and I would watch frustrating, appalling, patience-sapping games on TV then wait after the final whistle, 'To hear Ron's excuses.' Ron always delivered. And then he too was gone.

I was at senior school; boys-only. We all talked football, but several of the lads seemed more inspired by Saturday hooligans and bootboys than the exploits of any team, local or national; they followed and idolised the firms, the Casuals. The greatest excitement was generated by a TV documentary exposing the extremes of violence at games in England and featuring one 'Harry the Dog', who became more of a hero to some than any of the effete participants in the uniformed kickabout that the terrace thugs largely ignored. One schoomate worried me: he created pen-flick drawings of stadia, peopling them not with players balls, goals, but with fighters and weapons, modern gladiators; once again the deep, ancestral past revealed its relentless grip on our times. He drew stick-figures piling on stick-figures, flying fists like little maces, knuckledusters, headbutts, the flashing ply of knives; blood. Blood of course, most and best of all. And throughout he commentated on the melee, combining this with the *haaaaaaaaaaaa* battle-noises of a child mashing toy armies together into Armageddon; he was engaged, driven, energised beyond words. When he was told some-someone had insulted his colours, he put on a fine face of determination 'I'll *get* em.'

He was not an exception or outlier. He was the norm of the times.

Weeeee arreee the pride of the Midlands, the Cock of the North, we all hate Scousers and Geordies of course! Sweet schoolboy voices sang. You could *hear* them trying to muscle their way into manhood, to force their balls to drop. *We all hate Leeds and Leeds and Leeds/Leeds and Leeds and Leeds/And Leeds and Leeds and Leeds and Leeds/We all fuckin hate Leeds (etc ad infinitum)* To the tune of the Dambusters March.

Impiously and with impunity, they even raided the hymnal, the FA Cup anthem of old. *Redandwhiiii-ite, redandwhiiii-ite, we'll support you evermore...*

Boys who scorned choir practice learned the solidarity of singing en masse: comforting, hypnotic rhythm, scarf-swaying, the ability to lift spirits, energise winners, boost a flagging team, perhaps even summoning its own brand of magic to overturn imminent defeat. The rush of happy-hormones, the thrill of being one of the choir, exercising the delight of the voice raised in harmony; the feeling of belonging, not isolated, not just a note on a line but one of many, essential to the whole.

At the school, you were black-and-white or red-and-white, that or a foreigner, an enemy-within, a legitimate target. Before I started there, I was advised in hushed and earnest tones that, if challenged, to name my favourite team, I should recite a litany—*red-and-white-black-and-white-current-of-of-the-table-England.*

For my safety I should not reveal that I had long ago chosen claret-and-blue, based not on local loyalties or even football per se, but on liking the colours, which were at the very least chosen from a picture in a football annual. In the blackwhite-redwhite philosophy, it was wrong not to be a supporter, wrong, perhaps even worse, to be a 'part-time' supporter. A follower you had to be, following everywhere. The same sacred duty extended to backing England, no matter, wave the flag, sing the songs, no talking the team down, no defeatism, eyes and ears closed, gonnawin, mustwin, willwin; this was patriotism. To that group, I didn't let on about my cynicism for post-match excuses. But my patriotism was already degraded, holed, beginning in 1970 and worsening as time reeled on.

Timereel: 1982, the year we were going to get it right. We didn't. And *they* made a bloody dreadful record into the bargain.

Timereel: 1986. England, doing well (let's be fair),

put out of the contest by a talented player who, bluntly, cheated. He used his hand and not his head—oh yes he bloody did. My patriotism flared, as outrage. But remember—you must remember the values of the Corinthians, accept the ref's decision, swallow hard.

I grew more troubled. It cannot, just cannot, be 'my country, right or wrong', for that leads to blockhead groupthink, the mindless chants, the fist in the face, blood on the terraces. Supporting the team should be something more… sophisticated. In football as in any other form of patriotism, unthinking support is as outrageous as abandonment of one's country only to take up uncritical worship of another. Why reject the faults, the shame, the bad leaders of home only to adopt and legitimise the same elsewhere? In the early 70s, Big Jace sported a Brazil shirt; he liked them because they won. He put that shirt away when their streak came to an end and chose another. More than a decade later, people would yell *'Go and live in Russia!'* at me and friends as we staffed a Ban The Bomb stall on market days; they missed the point. You can criticise the home team without decamping entirely. True Patriots Ask Questions—Carl Sagan said that. But admittedly, he probably knew nothing about soccer.

Timereel to a brief stop-off at World Cup 1990: at least we had a decent song. Still lost, though. Fourth place, mind…

Timereel—1994. We failed to qualify for the World Cup. Again. Reel on.

Part of you summons faith in the team, we will win, we will win, we are three down and playing like cart horses, but we will prevail, any minute. Part of you is storming off, ripping up your ticket. How often do you have to be deflated, disappointed, punctured, provoked, enraged, before faith dies? For some, the answer is never, their redoubt is *redwhite-blackwhite-eeeeennngglannnnd!*

Flagwave-chant, conjure the rescuing magic or at least salve the hurt. Harmless hoping in some, prickly pride in others, and then, building resentment, lurking bitterness, anger, hate, scapegoat-hunting, all the way to xenophobic psychosis.

Timereel—to a tabloid headline heralding another England-Germany clash. Frontpage: 'Achtung! Surrender—For you Fritz, ze Euro 96 is over'; the faces of England players topped with poorly cut and worse-pasted tin hats; the clodhopping unfunniness, the tin-hatted tin-earedness, the sheer, horrible embarrassment of it. The icy-dead grip of the past on a nation that could not move on from either 1945 or 1966. For the first time, traitor thoughts strode into my mind: *I hope we lose. After this, we deserve to lose.*

I knew I could rely on my boys. It was the year football came home again—only to pack its traps quick as you like for another extended vacation.

Timereel further, through more penalty shootout disasters, Press obsession with WAGS and other irrelevant drivel, football is lost, obscured by trivia, expensive clothes, flashcash ostentation, entombed in money. As we hurtle forward, note the damaged, jagged pieces expelled in my wake: fragments of dead pride, burnt-out belief. The managers came, went again; each time the glory would return, it was bound to, and when it didn't, off went the boss—it was his fault. I recall a TV commentator openly sneering as one failed leader left the pitch after his final game; a real manager is taking over now, our troubles at an end—glory, glory, glory.

The team got worse. The glory-glory manager was gone within a year.

I have never felt such cold fear for my safety, my life even, as in the enforced company of football fans on a local-line train snake-clanking out of London. The clatter and thud of ageing rolling stock was drowned as they poured in from the narrow platform of forgottenwhichstation: there were no more than twenty, but they made the halloo of an army in battle-heat, war-hate. But these weren't exuberant schoolboys discovering the joys of communal singing, but grown men, shorthaired, tanked-up, angry sore losers who had been let down—now someone had to pay.

Ourteam-ourteam-ourteam-ourteam-ourteam-ourteam-otherteams-winningteamdie!

'No one even fuckin *look* at me or I'll *take* ya!' one addressed the carriage at large.

They filled the aisles, looming over us. The more comedic ones mugged and howled, using up excess rage-energy by tonguing their team's name, loyal, loud and proud, I supposed they thought themselves, but the threat of harm was brutal, razor-cold and real. Instinct thrummed: look up, but carefully. Is it all just noise? No—that one, that one and that one, they are ready to fight. Only it would not be a fight, just infliction of pain. It was akin to a hijack; when would the tension prove too much, when would they pick a victim, make an example?

'Does any cunt on this fuckin train want to try me? Well? Do ya? Fuckin do ya?'

His face was white, not red. Cold white drained-blood fury. His matchday hurt screamed for redress; he wanted to paint his love and loyalty in someone else's blood. He would doubtless do it for England too—for his country, it would be a sweet and fitting thing that someone else should die.

'C'mon mate, calm down, there's women and kids in here,' chided one of his mates in a mild tone.

'What do I fuckin care about that?' Wild gesticulation, lager-spilling.

The mild mate backed off, knowing he was lucky not to be treated summarily as a traitor to the cause. The passengers remained silent, tense, terrified, until the doors sighed open at anothercan'trememberstation and they shoved one another out, still gesturing, screaming, threatening, *Ourteam-ourteam-ourteam-ourteam-ourteam-ourteam-otherteams-winningteamdie!*

I wonder if those men—yes, all men—remember their display of loyalty that day, or was it just another Saturday to them, blurred recall of pumping veins, bunched fists, screwed-up faces, throats hoarse from chanting, bawling, promising pain? I was afraid of my own violent thoughts too: *What these people want is a war. May one come and take them.*

Watching England over the years was character-building; you cannot have what you want just because of who you are, what you are or where you're from. The world doesn't work that way and no amount of blind faith will correct the deficiency. Give it up. Once the 2010 World Cup came, I scowled, sulked, stationed myself resolutely out in the garden, refusing to come in to look at the games or hear the excuses. Do I have to detail the year's outcome? The little boy of the Mexico World Cup, his pure, innocent, baffled belief, had been left far behind.

Timereel to a very precise date and place: the twenty-seventh of June 2016; the main bar of the Queen's Arms. The pub always filled for matches, sometimes four or five TVs on, counting the bar and various nooks, but tonight we had only the big roll-down screen over the south-facing window, cinema-style projection of the latest game; England v Iceland. Naughty Pierre and I had found seats not too far from the bar, not too far from the screen; we had pints of Jaipur and Naughty Pierre's phone, my betting-slip.

'Are you sure you want to do this?' he was amused. 'You can cash out any time you want.' It was the first bet I had made in my entire existence, barring a joke flutter on a horse-race because one of the nags had the same name as my dog (it won); and yet I felt no danger of chance snatching away my stake. Tonight was to be a reckoning. As the game kicked off, I was in the distinctly odd situation of wanting England to win, wanting to lose my money, but the cold, implacable feeling remained that I wasn't going to lose—*they* were. No 'we' any longer. The disintegration of belief was complete. Poor little 1970 boy, stranded so far back in reeled time.

At 78 minutes, the commentator lobbed in that this game would be forgotten quickly by the rest of Europe; I, however, concurred with the online paper; 'this game' will be remembered and we will be mocked, *ad infinitum*.

'You're up to seventy quid,' Pierre waved the phone. 'Cash out?'

I dismissed the momentary temptation. England didn't look like scoring any time before Christmas.

'Eighty. It'll be too late to cash out soon.'

I felt safe, very safe. And only faintly disgusted with what I had become.

It became too late to cash out.

Three minutes' injury time added.

Full Time: England 1 Iceland 2: jeering, disgust, complaints, criticism, a mass retreat to the bar at the Queens, there were many sorrows to drown. From the TV, players foot-dragging, head-hanging from the pitch, chants of, *You're not fit to wear the shirt*—same tune as, *We'll support you evermore*.

Back to the online paper: *'They've been awful tonight and thoroughly deserved to lose.'*

'This is a total humiliation and their fans are letting them know in no uncertain terms that they're not best pleased with this result.'

'Their passing was awful, their deliveries were awful, they were bereft of ideas and gave the ball away cheaply. The manager is going to have some explaining to do in the

wake of this shambles and will surely be out of a job very, very soon.'

He was, less than half an hour after the whistle.

Another one gone.

A hundred pounds; it was a welcome windfall. I suppose as an act of treason it was distinctly downmarket; but that hundred was barely compensation for the waiting, the confused frustration, of a bemused little boy.

I wore my treason with ease and grace—and bought another pint for Naughty Pierre.

'Any further advice?'

Pierre sipped at his beer thoughtfully. 'Yeah. Stop gambling.'

Where The Past Belongs

Self-employed people should keep their financial records for at least five years, for tax purposes.

I returned from the South, once again without a job but this time with a plan; after seventeen years' experience of debt and benefit advice, I would share my accumulated wisdom, going to work for myself as a trainer, knowledgeable and good-humoured like The Expert, but also a mentor, a battler, an inspiration—*chapeau*, McLennan. I would steal some of their best lines too. Driven by economic and personal imperatives, this was a gamble; I was yet to benefit from the advice on that subject of Naughty Pierre.

I left my papers far longer than that sober five years; after a decade of glazed-over memory, I slid a large box from the back of a cupboard and set it down beside my newly acquired cross-cutting shredder, capable of rending six sheets at a time, wow, this baby is powerful, it can even shred CDs: the past, rearranged as ribbons; train tickets, documents, dockets, printouts, letters, bills, invoices, receipts.

(*Razzzz!*)

Copies of my Income Tax Self-Assessment forms; I

remembered the sheer teeth-grinding frustration of setting myself up as self-employed—bureaucracy, barriers, finding, filling, filing forms. I found the online system far easier to navigate, but the paperwork far more satisfying to destroy. My blue-backed accounts book, printouts of taxes charged, paid, and acknowledged, the letter marking the end of it all after a stale period of barren declarations, '*Nil-Nil-Nil*': 'You are no longer required to file Income Tax Self-Assessments'.

(*Razzzz!*)

My 2007 diary with its week-in week-out crossings-out of date, time, place; bookings ruined by Benjamin the Idiot. During his short but memorable reign at the Training Centre he would doubtlessly have described himself as 'dynamic', 'thrusting', 'cutting edge', and other words employed by fools to make themselves feel important. To stamp his authority on the Centre he called us all, trainers on various subjects from around the country, to the London head office to hear his statement, his muscle-flex manifesto. The Centre, he announced, was to increase its ambitions, extend its operations and so, of course, make more money. It would do so by booking more and more courses in venues nationwide. Benjamin would coordinate this expansion and we would all find ourselves very busy. As I had only recently started as a trainer and needed income soon, this sounded promising.

As Benjamin spoke, I saw the uncharacteristically gloomy look on Selina's face, his office manager. Known for her indefatigability, friendliness and efficiency, she usually made the London office a pleasure: however this time she was glum, wordless, shooting deadly looks at Benjamin as he reached his peroration. What was wrong? We were soon to find out. Controlled and confident, Benjamin told us he intended to institute regular quality checks on our work; feathers ruffled, especially among the very experienced trainers, but, so far, this seemed fair enough. This checking would be achieved, he said, 'By sending each of you to another trainers' course as a Mystery Shopper who will report back to me.' A long, stunned pause, and a gut-rumble of disbelief spread across the room. Selina sent a cannonade of hate towards her boss. Someone asked the obvious question: how can we be mystery shoppers on one another's courses when you've just called us all here, we've met, we know one another… Selina's expression told us this was just the beginning.

A little later, the diary dates began arriving: benefits courses, debt counselling, managing rent arrears, representation in court for non-lawyers. The year was filling up, I was due to travel to all sorts of places, the travel would cost me in advance but I'd get it back. I wrote and updated training packs and acetates, this work wasn't paid but it would be payday soon enough as I presented course after course, submitted invoices, claimed fees. It would be a fine, solid start to my self-employed career.

Selina called me. She shed her customary London tones for a fine but doom-laden patois. 'Shootim widda gon.'

I was about the tenth call, of the exact same sort, that she had been forced to make that day. Every training date in the coming month for every trainer had melted away, not confirmed but infirm.

I crossed out all my dates, put my diary aside, and hoped next month would be better.

But the call came.

'Shootim widda gon.'

The Idiot had mismanaged every date. All arrangements were pure ambition. There were no venues booked, no trainees, no work, no fees.

I tore the cardboard back off the diary, pulled the pages away from the spine and fed page after crossed-out page of my cancelled year into the chattering blades.

(*Razzzz!*)

The *Tax Credits—the problem areas* debacle was not Benjamin's fault, as it predated his reign of error. I had only just started as a self-employed trainer and needed the work; I took on this course reluctantly, and against my nagging better judgement. I knew the Tax Credit rules, but I wondered if I knew them to a sufficiently advanced level. I read the training pack—I had to update it but it was already written—and my confidence wobbled. There simply didn't seem to be much to it; in fact, its first half was the basic TC training course, and the second a bit more of the basics with few whistles and bells. No burning questions were raised or answered. The only complex content was a lengthy calculation: Tax Credits were calculated over

365 days, so what happens if your award runs for a shorter period, or if you have to calculate an award over a leap year?

Use a computer, was my short answer. The exercise was painful and the answer sheet provided for the trainer would have depressed Einstein. Reading this dense formula, my mind went back to chanted timestables, my life-long struggle with numbers. There was nothing for it, I would have to follow the answer sheet step-by-step until I understood it thoroughly. What a way to earn a bean.

The bloody answer sheet was ramblingly wrong. I patched it up as best I could, but from that moment I couldn't rest. The night before the course I barely slept, lopsided, ragged numbers kept running around my panicking head, never adding up, always reaching a different total.

'You've got a lovely lot in there today,' Selina enthused. 'Must be five of the best advisers in the country waiting for you!' I nearly ran for the train home. I should have. The day's beginning brought false confidence as the five best advisers in the country got the initial exercise wrong; the rest of the day closed around me in a cold-sweat shell as it became clear they *were* the best five advisers in the country and I was a shuddering, frightened fraud.

'There's been a complaint.' That was my greeting on my next visit to the training centre; the five were not impressed with either the course or the trainer. 'They said it didn't do what it said on the tin.'

'No, it bloody didn't. And *you* wrote it,' I snapped

back and stalked into the training room to teach the basic Tax Credits course, where I felt safe.

A few weeks later I agreed, with every instinct telling me *no*, to run the advanced course again, as there was no one else available. *No one daft enough*, I griped to myself. On arrival at the London training rooms, a damnfool feeling biting my heels, I found there were only two trainees—not the killer elite of the advice world but two pleasant charity workers without a single moment's training in Tax Credits. Relief gambolled with joy as I scrapped the advanced course and improvised a basic session that turned out, with two engaged and enthusiastic participants, to be one of the most enjoyable days of my short career as a trainer.

I never did the advanced course again.

The *Tax Credits—the problem areas* workbook and feverishly annotated trainer's answer sheet: gobble them down, hungry blades.

(Razzzz!)

Papers from meetings about 'financial inclusion'. Earnest discussions of helping people out of poverty by helping them take control, by simple means such as educating those who had never used one how to open a bank account, to write a cheque. We discussed basic bank accounts—no frills, no overdrafts, ideal for the broke, for recovering bankrupts who were otherwise ignored, excluded—but battled against the tide because although the banks agreed to provide the things, they operated a commercial *omerta*: they would never refer anyone to them unless the customer asked very specifically for a basic account. I wondered what the cool-hall dignitaries of the Ironmarket Bank would have made of it all.

At the end of a hopeful talking-shop day, we were asked, round-robin, for closing comments. 'Let's make sure,' I said slowly, 'That we are not here in a year's time discussing the exact same points.'

Looks of irritation. Of course we wouldn't. Away, cynic. Twenty years later I would be back in similar meetings.

Agendas, notes, bulletins, plans, handouts, memories of the chilly stares.

(Razzzz!)

I arrived at one of the few substantial dates arranged by Benjamin the Idiot; there was a venue, my word, there were trainees! But he had tricks up his sleeve. I had updated the training pack, but it was London's job to do the print run and send completed packs to the venue; you brought your notes and acetates for the overhead projector, collected the box of packs, handed them out and taught. The training room resembled the assembly hall of a school scheduled for demolition in about 1950; it was basic, cold, uncomfortable. The trainees sat at their inkwell desks and waited.

The subject was the brand-new Employment and Support Allowance, and I began as usual. 'Governments of various stripes have, over the years, had the same idea about benefits for people who are sick or disabled: 'They're too easy to get, there are too many people on them and they stay on them too long.'

Everyone, they say, no matter how sick, should take up their bed and work. Each of these governments then has a bright idea: "Hey, why has no one thought of this before? We'll abolish the current benefits, replace them with an all-singing, all-dancing new benefit that ensures only those who are *genuinely* sick can get it, those who can go back to work get help to do so, and the help is targeted on those who need it." In 1995, the government had this flash of revelation and replaced Invalidity Benefit with Incapacity Benefit. And now, in 2008, another government has the same flash of revelation, and Incapacity Benefit gets canned and here comes ESA. Here's a prediction: within a few years, another government will come along and say, "Hey, this ESA is too easy to get, there are too many people on it and they stay on it too long." There will be a flash of revelation and…'

Next, I would say, 'Let's see how ESA actually works.' This time, however, this wasn't possible: the packs from London had not arrived; I had acetates but there was no overhead projector; there was a flipchart easel but no pens, and into the bargain there was no flipchart paper either. The administrators at the venue spread their hands *who-me* fashion. The London training centre promised to check what had happened to the packs.

Hot and harassed, I limped the session through to the coffee break and made calls. Nobody knew where the packs were. They had forgotten to request a projector. My forehead was burning, but I thought it was just embarrassment; my nose began to run.

Returning to the room, I heard a trainee on her mobile. 'He's really, really unhappy. There's no materials, he can't do the course and, what's more, I don't think he's well.'

I sniffled, sneezed; my head and then my body turned hot-cold-hot-cold, on-off, on-off. I waited a little, but no packs arrived; I gathered the group, apologised, gave up, packed up, headed home. I was in bed with flu for days. I couldn't blame Benjamin for the flu, but the rest was his idiocy.

Invoice for travel costs and abortive training session—I charged for the full day and the fool was lucky I didn't add a surcharge—into the machine.

(Razzzz!)

Benjamin's last stand. He had booked multiple trainers into a large London venue to 'showcase' the training centre. Each of us was asked to present a short version of our introductory courses, and if we impressed, further bookings would flow from there. I was to do the debt course, which was normally great fun; I was known as 'the trainer who throws himself to the floor', owing to my one-man dramatization of Mr and Mrs Saxon's day in court. But, as you have probably guessed, Benjamin had done it again. We had been told to prepare our basic courses, but the venue and the trainees had been promised advanced, detailed training, they were experienced staff.

I phoned Benjamin's representative on earth. 'Find out who needs introductory and who needs advanced,' came the advice. 'Split them into two groups and teach two different sessions.'

'There is just one of me here. How do you propose I do that?'

'Well you could…'

'Thought so.'

The disastrous day played out, the only satisfaction afforded to me being the chance to correct a bumptious solicitor over whether a situation called for an application on an N244 or N245. Don't ask.

Every scrap of my final humiliation at bumbling Benjamin's hands:

(Razzzz!)

The London training centre had geographical problems too. Post-Idiot, I was booked to travel somewhat further east than I would usually go, for a two-day course, and I needed to charge for hotel accommodation.

'We won't pay. You're in Derby, the venue is only an hour away from you.'

'I'm in Derby*shire*. By train, I'm no less than three hours away from Derby. And four from your venue. I like sitting reading my book, but not for *that* long after a day's work.'

'Oh, sorry. We don't know much outside London. Perhaps we should get a map.'

'Perhaps you should.'

I was then booked on a two-day session in Sunderland and the same performance took place.

'You can get there easily, you're in the North.'

'The distance from here to Sunderland is greater than here to London.'

'Oh.'

'Map.'

'Oh. Yes.'

When I got to Sunderland and kicked off the course, dread gripped me: I was in another training room of people who knew more than me. It was an introductory benefits course, but it was plain nobody needed that. I was assured that the training was just what they wanted, taken as a refresher and updater, and it was my good fortune I had never met a nicer group of people on my travels. We enjoyed a lovely couple of days kicking ideas around and having a laugh; they were also the only group to take me out for a drink and meal in the evening. I did a second session with them a while later, and I'm still in contact with a couple of them.

Train tickets to Sunderland (via Newcastle, on to the Metro; the London people weren't the only ones geographically confused, I thought Sunderland was North of Newcastle, ooops), hotel receipts (the Travelodge, the Roker Hotel), course notes, invoices.

(Razzzz!)

I had a very comfortable relationship with Seat H2 on the London to Manchester train. It was right by the sliding door as you entered the train, one seat on its own with a little table, cup and saucer, a glass and a knife and fork swaddled in a clean white napkin, all waiting for me bathed in the soft yellow light of my own table lamp as I tottered on the train after my day's training, whether good or bad. At that time if you booked early or, if you were more of a risk-taker, you waited until the last moment, you could travel First Class for less than the price of a Standard ticket. It was a crazy system, but why ignore it when I could get Seat H2 and travel home in splendid isolation, with tea or coffee, biscuits, a light dinner and a glass of wine served at-seat: bliss. The promise of escape in Seat H2, a quiet coach without interruptions from phones and phone-heads and a fast, comfortable journey home soothed my jangling nerves sufficiently to save Benjamin's worthless life on several occasions. I could relax, read, ponder, sleep, forget a bad day or replay the highlights of a triumph.

The staff were helpful and, on occasion, more than, when my top-up of red wine consisted of most of the bottle, for instance, or once, on a near-empty Coach H, a whole bottle was handed to me as we pulled out of Stoke station. I made a vague 'share' gesture at the only other person I could see, but he waved me down, smiled and said, 'Make me proud, son.' I did, and as we came into Manchester Piccadilly the occupant of Seat H2 was feeling, as my Dad would have said, 'very pleased with the world.'

Four years on London-Manchester trains in Seat H2.

(Razzzz!)

The last training course. The very last. Tax Credits again, Birmingham. The day went well; it wasn't the memory of the course, the venue or the trainees that needed to be purged, but the nasty, life-changing surprise awaiting me at home.

(Someone leaves, someone falls ill…)

Accursed day. Forget it all, obliterate.

(Razzzz!)

Papers, papers, papers; house sale, house rental; job applications un-responded to, ignored, brief rejection letters, flashbacks to the giro days; court papers, demands, arguments, decrees. I was in no mood to play remember-when, but I couldn't help visions of Judge Renfrew, frowning in concentration, plying his regretful pen, 'That is all I can do.'

And this is what I can do.

(Razzzz!)

The loan contract (Regulated by The Consumer Credit Act 1974) and entire correspondence with The Caring Bank, including the letter in which they upheld my complaint of poor service and said they would 'offer words of advice to members of our staff'. And with it the clinging habit I observed in my one-time clients and which I acquired, of the shiver of fear as an envelope lands on the mat, the terror of what lies within.

(Razzzz!)

There is no such thing as the past; there is an ongoing, unstoppable sequence of present moments, from which you can scrape fragments as they pass by, arrange them as suits your delusions and dignify them with the title 'memory'. This is, however, a mistake; we retain keepsakes at our peril. Photographs, letters, certificates, mementoes, receipts, every fluttering one, into the strong cross-cutting jaws. Wipe the slate, be done with what's gone, break its grip; be free, live on.

Tabula. *(Razzzz!)*

Ingram Content Group UK Ltd.
Milton Keynes UK
UKHW011459270423
420882UK00023B/284